17

4 WEEKS

Please Don't Lose the Date Card

CONCORD
FREE PUBLIC LIBRARY

Concord, Massachusetts

LEAPING BEAUTY
✧ and other animal fairy tales ✧

A gift from
the
Lois and Robert Evans, Jr.
Children's Book Fund

Concord Free
Public
Library

LEAPING
BEAUTY

✧ and other animal fairy tales ✧

GREGORY
MAGUIRE

ILLUSTRATED BY *Chris L. Demarest*

HARPERCOLLINS*PUBLISHERS*

Maguire

Library of Congress Cataloging-in-Publication Data

Maguire, Gregory.

Leaping Beauty : and other animal fairy tales / Gregory Maguire ; illustrated by Chris L. Demarest.—1st ed.

p.   cm.

ISBN 0-06-056417-2 — ISBN 0-06-056418-0 (lib. bdg.)

1. Fairy tales. 2. Children's stories. [1. Fairy tales. 2. Animals—Fiction. 3. Short stories.] I. Demarest, Chris L., ill. II. Title.

PZ8.M2826Le 2004   2003024083

398.24'5—dc22

[F]

Typography by Nicole de las Heras

1   2   3   4   5   6   7   8   9   10

❖

First Edition

This book is for
Luke, Alex, and Helen—
my own leaping beauties.

CONTENTS

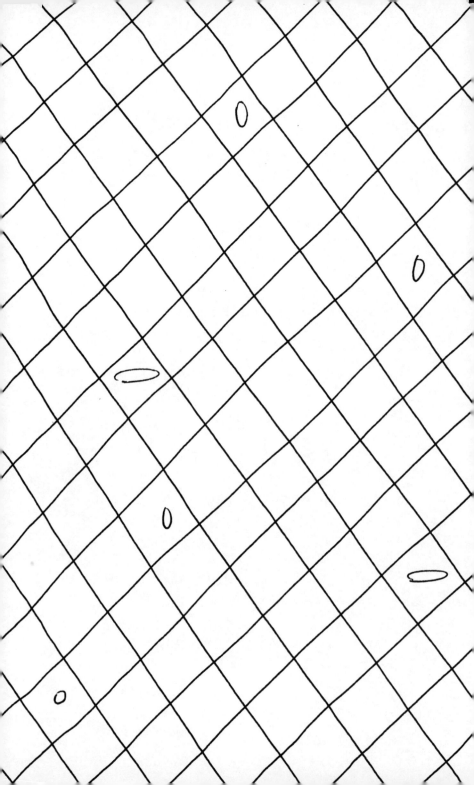

LEAPING BEAUTY

The king and queen of the frogs gave birth to a baby. They were delighted, for they had long wanted a child. The tadpole was as green as the slime in a vernal pond, and the bumps on her skin had bumps of their own. The king and queen decided to call her Beauty, as she was the most beautiful thing they had ever seen.

When the time came to have a party to celebrate her birth, the royal parents invited all the fairies in the kingdom, including bumblebees, butterflies, and an airborne brotherhood of beetles.

The party started out swell. The bumblebees brought their bagpipes, the butterflies brought their banjos, and the beetles brought their bassoons. The queen frog set up the guests in a summerhouse so that their hootenanny music could carry across the pond.

(You'd be surprised how much music is written for bagpipe, banjo, and bassoon trios.)

The king frog kept a watch fondly over his little Beauty.

The bumblebees ate the biscuits, the butterflies ate the butter and bread, and the beetles ate the beets. The queen frog kept putting out more, for it was her fondest hope that the fairies would feel like bestowing precious gifts on her beloved, wide-smiled daughter.

When dinner was through, the music struck up again. Many of the fairies danced the hootchy-cootchy. As the lights began to dim and evening chill settled in the air, one by one the fairies stopped their dancing and playing and came forward to look lovingly upon the newborn frog.

"On behalf of the bumblebees, I have a gift," said the boss of the bumblebees, chomping on his cigar. "We bees like to hum a lot. We love songs. So let this little cutie hum and sing songs whenever she likes. She will have a beautiful voice for all to hear and enjoy. Her *ribbit* will be as loud as a foghorn."

"Thank you," murmured the queen frog. "Thank you all, my darling bees."

The baron of the butterflies fluttered forward. "On behalf of all the butterflies, I should like to give her a gift," he said. "I should like her to move with the grace of a butterfly. Her froggy progress through a pond shall be as moonlight through a glade."

"Bravo," chortled the king frog. "Dear butterflies— our unending thanks!"

Just then there was a buzz at the end of the field. Who should come droning along but the wickedest fairy of the meadows—a huge, ancient hornet, with a stinger as long as a candy cane.

"Who invited *her*?" muttered the queen frog.

"Croaked if I know," her husband muttered back. "Thinks she can just crash any party she wants? I'll give her a piece of my mind!" He opened his mouth and unrolled his long, sticky tongue, flexing it threateningly.

"Careful, my dear," said his wife. "She *is* the most powerful fairy in the field. She stings you, you'll be croaking the Last Big Croak. I suppose we ought to give her a piece of cake or something." She put on her brightest face. "Well, look who's here to grace our little party! Old Dame Hornet, what a surprise!"

"You rude things," cried Old Dame Hornet in a rage. "You have a party and invite all these simpering bugs, and you forget to invite *me*? I'm rocking with fury! I'm rolling with rage! I'll give your daughter a little present to remember this insult by!"

With a speed surprising for one so old and frail, Old Dame Hornet flung herself to the cradle and looked down into the face of the pretty

little baby frog. "Before your first birthday," she cried, "you shall bite down on a stray explosive from some stupid human engineering project, and you shall blow yourself to smithereens!" And she gave a fiendish cackle.

"Oh, anything but that!" shrieked the queen frog. She fell into a dead faint, which made a loud slapping noise in the water, like a belly flop.

But the bishop of the beetles, who had been sneaking a little extra nectar at the refreshment table, now came forward. "I haven't given our gift to the little princess yet," he said. "On behalf of the beetles, I declare that you shan't blow yourself up when you bite down on a stray explosive. You'll just begin to cry, because it will hurt. You will wail, you will moan, you will splash yourself with tears. We will all call you Weeping Beauty. It will be dreadfully sad, but at least you'll still be alive."

"Curses!" shrieked the hornet. "Well, crying all the time, that's pretty bad too. I liked the exploding frog idea better, but you can't win them all. Ta ta, everybody. And next time," she hissed, "*invite me to the party.*"

Recovering from her fit of vapors, the queen joined the king in saying good-bye to the bumblebees and butterflies and beetles. Then hired bedbugs came in to turn down the sheets so the king and queen could go to sleep. Worried to distraction, though, the frog parents couldn't sleep.

"Our Beauty will have a voice," said the king, trying to be consoling. "She'll have grace in motion."

"She'll weep—that's her fate!" said the queen, who began to weep herself, in sympathy.

The queen and king did their best to protect little Beauty. They watched over her night and day. Beauty seemed such a pretty little thing, gifted at singing and dancing. She was always happy. Everyone around her was cheered up by the crooning of her second contralto voice, by her impromptu tap dancing and soft-shoe routines.

But though show business was gratifying, Beauty longed to be alone from time to time. She didn't want always to be the solo act in frog society. She wanted a break.

So one evening a week or two later, Beauty slipped away through the grass when no one was looking. She had never paddled in the river by herself, and she enjoyed what she saw: the beetles in their holes, the bees in their trees, the butterflies fluttering by in the wind.

Then she saw a metal box drifting in the strong current in the middle of the river. It looked a little bit like an iron sandwich, with cables and cords trailing out of the middle like stringy bits of raw onion.

Beauty felt a powerful hunger. She swam over and took a huge bite.

Ow! It felt like a volcano in her mouth. It tasted like lava lasagna. It seared the roof of her tongue and made her teeth ache.

Naturally enough, Beauty began to cry. Huge tears formed in her eyes and rolled down her nose. She was only barely able to make it to the riverbank. She tried to call out for her mother and father, but all she could do was weep—loudly. Since her voice was strong from all that singing, her parents heard the racket, and they came hopping as quickly as their old quaking legs could propel them.

Now, her parents weren't king and queen of the frogs for nothing. They were intelligent frogs. They picked up their ailing, flailing, wailing baby Beauty and brought her to the base of the oak tree where Old

Dame Hornet had a little nest.

There, Beauty cried. Morning, noon, and night. Her parents took turns feeding her, but she cried even when she was being fed. She was noisy, and she got noisier with practice. She made a sound like a fire engine going past, going past, going past, but never going away.

Old Dame Hornet was furious. She flew out of her nest and came down to yell at the baby to shut up. "Can't you rock that little pollywog to sleep or something?" she said.

"I'm afraid not," said the king frog. "She's crying so hard she can't fall asleep."

Old Dame Hornet liked her little nest too much to move. She had fixed it up just right, with a picture of her first-grade teacher on the wall and a braided rug on the floor. So she flew off to see the bishop of the beetles. The bishop's secretary saw her into the bishop's study.

"You gave a gift to that pollywog—that she would not die when she bit on an explosive, but that she would weep and weep. Now you must take that gift away from the child," cried Old Dame Hornet. "She's making an unholy racket."

"I'm not an unreasonable beetle," said the bishop. "But you're far too quick to the sting, Old Dame Hornet. If you get over your anger and apologize to little Beauty and promise never to hurt her again, I'll say a blessing over her. Maybe she'll stop crying."

"Her parents didn't invite me to the party," said Old Dame Hornet. "I never get invited anywhere. It makes me mad all over again just to think about it. I'm not going to promise anything, Your Eminence. I don't bargain with clergy. Besides, I like to be mean. It's fun."

Off she flew to interfere with the baron of the butterflies.

"Can you do me a favor, Your Excellency?" she said. "That little Beauty is weeping too hard. I can't stand it. Can you say a spell of your own and make her stop weeping?"

"I don't know much about weeping," said the

baron. "Butterflies don't weep. But we spend a lot of time sleeping in our cocoons before we become so gorgeous. Maybe I could change the spell from weeping to sleeping. It's simply a spelling change, after all, from *w* to *sl*. *Weeping* to *sleeping*."

"Do it," said Old Dame Hornet.

"What'll you pay me?" he said.

"Your Excellency, I'll sting you if you don't," she said. "Excellently."

The baron of the butterflies knew that her stinger would puncture his beautiful wing and cripple him for life. He was a good fairy, but he was a little vain. So he meandered over to Weeping Beauty in as direct a route as he could manage, being a butterfly.

"Maybe it'll be better if she sleeps a little," he said to the king and the queen of the frogs. "You need some rest too."

"We'll never rest till this spell is lifted off our one and only child," they said.

The baron of the butterflies said a spell and changed *Weeping* to *Sleeping*. Instantly the little frog stopped wailing and sobbing and began to sleep. Boy, did she sleep. She snored so loudly that it sounded like a chain saw buzzing through the oak tree.

When Old Dame Hornet came along and saw what had happened, she was relieved—at first. She took herself to bed with a hot toddy and a copy of *TV Guide*. But she couldn't concentrate. Little Sleeping Beauty snored like thunder, louder than ever. Old Dame Hornet tried to sleep. But little Sleeping Beauty snored like competing kettledrum quartets having a battle of the bands during a thunderstorm. Thunder and landslides and rock bands and kettledrums. It was just awful. Old Dame Hornet pulled her braided rug up over her head.

Soon the wicked old fairy could stand it no longer. Off she zizzed to see the boss of the bumblebees.

"That Weeping Beauty has become Sleeping Beauty, and it's worse than ever!" she cried. "I can get no rest, neither day nor night! You're a bumblebee. Are you a spelling bee? Can you change the spell, Your Effervescence?"

"No can do, tootsie," said the boss of the bumble-bees, who had a little sting of his own and therefore wasn't so scared of Old Dame Hornet.

"Please," said Old Dame Hornet.

"What's the payoff if I do?" said the boss of the bumblebees.

"What do you want as a payment?" asked Old Dame Hornet, in as fetching a manner as she could manage given she was quivering with exhaustion and rage.

The boss of the bumblebees buzzed in thought. At last he said, "Listen, you Old Dame, this is my fee. You aren't to put any more evil spells on little babies. You know why you never get invited to birthday parties? Because you're a nasty piece of work. Try being a little nicer. Maybe you'll get asked out more often."

"I like being a crank," screamed Old Dame Hornet, but she thought some more about what the boss of the bumblebees was saying. She said in a quieter voice, "Are you asking me on a date?"

"That's my payment," said the boss of the bumblebees.

"For an old dried-up hornet, you've kept your looks pretty well, honeypot."

Old Dame Hornet wanted to sting him to death on the spot, but she needed his help. She simply gulped and said, "Well, maybe I'll go out for a stroll with you some evening. But if you try whispering sweet nothings in my ear, you'll *be* a sweet nothing sooner than you can say *concrete boots*."

"Fair's fair," said the boss of the bumblebees, chomping on the end of his cheroot. And he navigated over to see Sleeping Beauty. He could tell where she was because the entire oak tree above her was trembling with the force of her colossal snores.

Old Dame Hornet followed. At the door of her nest she turned and waited.

"Pick you up at eight P.M. sharp," the boss of the bumblebees said to the hornet. "Wear your red dancing shoes, darling."

"Humph!" buzzed Old Dame Hornet.

The boss of the bumblebees said a spell. He changed the frog from Sleeping Beauty to Leaping Beauty.

"There," he said to her doting parents, who were looking pretty bleary eyed by now, "this is as close to her normal self as she's likely to get."

Sleeping Beauty woke up and became Leaping Beauty. She bounded up in the air like a rubber ball, just about as high as the door to Old Dame Hornet's home.

Sadly, when the boss of the bumblebees broke the spell of the baron of the butterflies, the old spell of the bishop of the beetles kicked in again. So as Leaping Beauty leapt, she wept. She screamed like any baby who has just woken up from a nap. The sound came right up to Old Dame Hornet's doorway and went away again, like an ambulance driving by, and driving right back. Like an ambulance going up and down the street, hour after hour.

"I can't bear this!" cried Old Dame Hornet. "Weeping Beauty, Sleeping Beauty, Leaping Beauty! Get this little pollywog out of my life! Besides, every time she goes leaping by, her tears splash over my threshold and my braided rug is getting drenched!"

The boss of the bumblebees flew by holding a bunch of black-eyed Susans. "Flowers for Old Dame Hornet," he said. "Come on, sugarlips, let's paint this town black and yellow."

"Not till I settle this matter," she said. "I've seen the error of my ways. I've been a bad old hornet." She zizzed down to where the king and the queen of the frogs were waiting, with a dizzy look in their glazed eyes. "I give up, you win," she cried. "I'll never harm the child! I don't care if I never get invited to another birthday party! Take her away and let her grow up to be a normal frog! With my blessing."

"We thought you might agree, sooner or later," said the king and queen of the frogs. "Your Eminence, come here."

The bishop of the beetles, who had been hiding behind a fern, came forward. He said, "So do you agree never to pester this little froglet again?"

"I never want to *see* her again!" cried Old Dame Hornet.

"Cross your stinger and hope to die?"

"Honest promise and keep the change!" screeched the hornet.

So the bishop of the beetles took the weeping spell off Beauty. And the sleeping spell of the baron of the butterflies had already been revoked. But the boss of the bumblebees said, "She might as well stay Leaping Beauty. Leaping well never hurt a frog."

The pretty little tadpole kept her gorgeous looks

for her whole life. She was always as green as slime, and the bumps on her bumps developed their own bumps. Furthermore, with her lovely long legs, she became a renowned hoofer and was a great success.

Once the boss of the bumblebees and Old Dame Hornet went on a date to see the fabulous star perform in a ballet. Old Dame Hornet was so moved by Leaping Beauty's talent that she tossed a bunch of roses on the stage.

Leaping Beauty bowed most graciously. Then she leaped all the way from the stage into the second balcony and gave Old Dame Hornet a kiss.

The ancient thing melted into happy tears and said, "You'd never be so good if I hadn't blessed you when you were born, my dear. I'm so proud of you I could sting myself to death!"

The king and queen of the frogs, applauding from the royal box across the theater, murmured fondly, "Oh, don't do that!" Then they invited Old Dame Hornet back to the Lily Pad Palace for a light refreshment. But the old fairy declined, and the boss of the bumblebees flew her home.

There she said good night and went inside to write in her journal. The silence at the bottom of the oak tree was gratifying, and so were her memories of the evening.

GOLDIEFOX AND THE THREE CHICKENS

There were once three chickens who lived in a house in the forest.

Papa Rooster was vain and short-tempered. Mama Hen was soothing and patient. Baby Chick was tired of being the littlest one all the time. "Why don't you go to the store?" he used to say to Mama Hen. "Can't you buy me a new little brother or sister?"

One morning all three chickens woke up in a bad mood.

Papa Rooster said, "My bed is so high, I almost fell on my beak jumping off the mattress this morning."

Mama Hen said, "Poor thing. My bed is so low, while I was asleep I rolled right off it and smack into my knitting needles."

Baby Chick said, "You think you have troubles! My bed is too small! I'm bumping into the headboard and the footboard! I need a new one! I know: Why don't we look in a catalog and order a new baby? Then we could give my little baby bed to my new brother or sister."

"I'll think about it, dear," said Mama Hen, which Baby Chick knew full well really meant, *Not very likely in this lifetime, honey chile.*

Mama Hen made some oatmeal and brought it to the table.

"Yikes, it's piping hot!" yelled Papa Rooster.

"So is mine," wailed Baby Chick.

"What a pair of complainers," said Mama Hen. "So blow on it to cool it down already."

"I prefer to save my breath for complaining," said Papa Rooster.

Baby Chick blew on his breakfast a little too hard, and then Papa Rooster had something to complain *about.* He didn't enjoy oatmeal in his coxcomb.

After they had all cleaned up, Mama Hen said, "Why don't we go for a walk in the forest and give the oatmeal a chance to cool down? Ourselves, too."

"I'll lead the way, as I'm the largest and most important," crowed Papa Rooster. "Also I have a wonderful sense of direction."

"I'll follow along behind, as I'm the last, the smallest, worth nothing at all," whimpered Baby Chick. "I wish I had a baby brother or sister chick that I could be bigger than. Let's hunt for one in the ferns."

"I'll go to the park and feed the ducks by myself if you two don't quit your bellyaching," said Mama Hen. And off they went into the woods, single file.

They were gone a long time because Papa Rooster's

sense of direction wasn't quite as wonderful as he thought.

Now, who should come slinking through the woods from the other direction but a golden fox. He was beautiful to behold, shiny as the foil around fancy chocolates. But he was miserable, for he had just been fired from his job as a carpenter at the local furniture store. It seemed that a lot of the customers were scared to order rocking chairs for their grannies or cradles for their new babies from a fox who was walking around with a sharp-toothed saw. Besides, he had sharp teeth of his own, which were big and in very good condition. Customers didn't like to come inside the shop.

The out-of-work carpenter—whose name was Goldiefox—was in a bad mood when he came upon the house of the three chickens. He smelled the smell of something delicious. He knocked on the door to ask if he could have a bite, for he was very hungry. When no one answered, he pushed the door open and looked inside.

He saw the table with three bowls of oatmeal. "My

word!" he said. "A delicious breakfast, and no one here to eat it."

Goldiefox took a spoonful of oatmeal from the largest bowl. "It is too hot," he said, and moved on to the medium-sized bowl. "It is too cold," he said. The smallest bowl had only a little oatmeal at the bottom, as most of it seemed to have been blown out all over the tablecloth. "This is just right," said Goldiefox, and ate what little there was. But he was still hungry, and he was still cross.

He went into the next room looking for a pie or a sandwich or something. There he saw three chairs. "Perhaps I'll take a rest and wait for the owners of this house to come home," he said to himself. He sat down on the largest chair. It was too hard. By now Goldiefox was thoroughly annoyed, and though he ought to have counted to ten and had a time-out, he lost his temper. He jumped up and down on the large, hard chair, and he broke it.

He then sat in the medium-sized chair. It was too soft. He jumped up and down on it and he broke it, too.

There was a small chair. Goldiefox tried to sit in it, but it was too small. Then he tried to jump up and down on it and break it, but it got stuck on his foot. It was a *very* small chair.

"This is not a good day," said Goldiefox to himself. "First I get fired from my job, then I get my foot stuck in a tiny chair. What next?"

Since the family still wasn't showing up, Goldiefox clumped upstairs to try to find a saw with which to remove the small chair from his foot. He found no work tools, but he did see a very high bed.

Since he was tired from all his jumping up and down and breaking furniture, he decided to have a nap. He tried to leap up on the high bed, and he smashed his face on the headboard and broke off a front tooth. We all have days like this sometimes.

Goldiefox became irate. He jumped up and down on the high bed and he broke it.

Next he found a very low bed. It was so low that it was hard to jump up and down on and break, so he threw it out the window.

Finally he found an exceedingly small bed. It was clearly too small for a fox to sleep in, but by now he was out of control. Goldiefox tried to jump up and down on it and break it, but the very small bed got stuck on his other foot.

Just at this moment the chicken family came home from their walk.

They were in bad moods. Papa Rooster pretended he hadn't gotten lost. Mama Hen pretended she couldn't hear any whining and walked straight into the kitchen. Baby Chick pretended he belonged to another family and had nine brothers and sisters.

Goldiefox heard them coming. Quite suddenly he found himself ashamed of his bad behavior. He hid in a convenient cupboard on the stair landing.

Papa Rooster looked in his bowl and said, "I'm ready for my breakfast, but it looks as if someone has been eating my oatmeal."

Mama Hen came out of the kitchen and looked in her bowl. "Someone has been eating *my* oatmeal," she said.

Baby Chick said, "Someone has been eating my

oatmeal, whatever I didn't blow all over the room by mistake! And there's nothing left for me!"

"What kind of a loony would break into our house and eat our oatmeal?" said Papa Rooster. "Let us investigate. I'll go first as I'm the strongest and the bravest."

"I'll go last as I'm the weakest and least important," said Baby Chick, for once glad to be the smallest.

"I'll call the cops," said Mama Hen. "Let the professionals do their jobs."

Papa Rooster strutted into the parlor. "Someone has been sitting in my chair! And he's jumped up and down on it and broken it!"

"Why do you assume it's a he?" said Mama Hen. "Maybe it's a she. I sometimes feel like jumping up and down on things and breaking them. But I choose to control my temper when I feel like that. It's my best quality, patience."

Then she saw her own chair and lost her patience. "Someone's been jumping up and down on my chair, and she's broken it!" she clucked, flabbergasted. "Though, thinking it over some more, it's probably a he."

"Someone's been jumping up and down on *my* chair," screamed Baby Chick, "and I can't even tell if it's *broken* because it isn't even *here* anymore!"

"This is serious," said Papa Rooster. "Everybody stay back. I'm going to look upstairs. I have a feeling whoever has done these foul deeds is still here."

"Oooh, I'm scared," said Baby Chick. "This is better than a horror movie."

Papa Rooster climbed the stairs to the bedrooms. Mama Hen and Baby Chick huddled close behind him.

"Somebody has been sleeping in my bed, and he jumped up and down on it and broke it!" cried Papa Rooster. "Not that I care very much. That bed is so high, it makes me dizzy trying to get down every morning."

"That's why you're always in such a bad mood," clucked Mama Hen. "If you had a better night's sleep, dear, you wouldn't be such a grouch all the time." She then looked for her bed. "My word! Someone's been sleeping on my bed, and it isn't even here!"

"There it is," said Baby Chick, looking out the window. "It's in the garden, squashing the squashes."

"If I catch that vandal, I'll give him a piece of my mind!" squawked Mama Hen. "Clearly he doesn't have any of his own."

"Why do you assume it's a he?" asked Papa Rooster, but Mama Hen was giving him such a look that he didn't wait for an answer.

"Someone's been jumping up and down on *my* bed, and it's probably broken or thrown out the window, but I can't even *find* it!" cried Baby Chick.

"We have problems with our furniture," said Papa Rooster.

"Do you think it could be ghosts?" said Mama Hen.

"What if it's hiding in the convenient cupboard on the stair landing?" screeched Baby Chick.

His parents looked at him.

"Well, that's where *I* hide when *I* do something wrong," he said.

The three chickens approached the door to the convenient cupboard on the stair landing. "Stand back," said Papa Rooster. "I'll fling the door open with a bold and decisive gesture."

"I'll henpeck to within an inch of his life anyone who's in there," scolded Mama Hen.

"Maybe it's a new baby brother or sister for *me*!" cried Baby Chick.

"Son, we have to have a little chat," said Papa Rooster. "However convenient a cupboard is, it's not where new baby brothers or sisters come from." He flung open the door.

Goldiefox, who had been trembling in terror at the sound of the furious chickens, stumbled out onto the landing. He tried to run away, but with a tiny bed on one foot and a tiny chair on the other, he merely tumbled to the bottom of the stairs.

In an instant the three chickens had launched themselves through the air and tackled him. Papa Rooster sat on his head. Mama Hen sat on his tail. Baby Chick ran around in the front and looked him in the eye.

"I can smell oatmeal on his breath!" he shouted. "This is our villain!"

"How dare you jump up and down on our furniture and break it!" cried Papa Rooster. "Would you like me to jump up and down on your head and break *that*?"

"How dare you throw my bed out the window!"
cried Mama Hen. "Would you like me to throw *you*
out the window?"

"How dare you eat my oatmeal, after I had blown
on it to cool it down!" cried Baby Chick. "Would you
like me to blow on you to cool *you* down?" Without
waiting for an answer, he made good on his threat.

"Please," said Goldiefox, "please. Dear chickens of the woods. I have been a bad fox. I have done everything wrong. I am out of work, I am hungry, and I have miniature furniture stuck to my feet. Furthermore I have broken a tooth as well as most of your furniture. This is not one of my good days. Do not jump up and down on me. Do not throw me out the window. And stop blowing in my face; it's very annoying."

Baby Chick stopped.

"I will tell you something," said Goldiefox. "If you let me live with you, I will build you all new furniture. The chairs will not be too hard or too soft or too little. The beds will not be too high or too low or too little. Perhaps I can set up shop in the backyard and make furniture there, away from the prying eyes of animals too frightened to buy furniture from me. You can sell it in your front room."

"Well, perhaps," said Papa Rooster. "I wouldn't be in such a bad mood if I could get a better night's sleep."

"If you got a better night's sleep, we'd *all* get a better night's sleep," said Mama Hen. "I think it's a great idea. Perhaps I'll make up batches of oatmeal and we can have an oatmeal restaurant, too. For all the customers who come to buy furniture."

"But where will you sleep?" asked Baby Chick.

"I can sleep in the convenient cupboard on the stair landing," said Goldiefox.

And that's just what they did. They opened a new store in the woods, called The Three Chickens Furniture

Store and Oatmeal Restaurant. Every once in a while the oatmeal was too hot to eat, so the chickens went for a walk in the woods. But they left Goldiefox behind to guard their house. With his broken front tooth, he was quite a scary-looking animal. So they never had trouble with hungry, destructive trespassers again.

Baby Chick never *did* get a baby brother or sister. But at the end of the day, when the carpenter tools were all stored away, Goldiefox would wash his face of sawdust and play with Baby Chick.

They especially enjoyed jumping on the furniture, now that it was strong enough to stand up to such punishment.

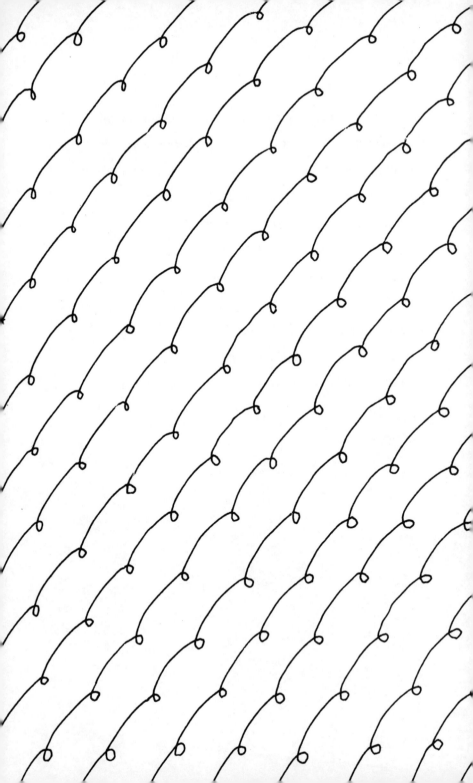

HAMSTER
AND GERBIL

Once there was a happy family who lived in a beaver dam. Not surprisingly, they were beavers. That is, the father and the mother were beavers. The children were adopted. There was a boy named Hamster and a girl named Gerbil. Not surprisingly, they were a hamster and a gerbil. Hamster was the hamster, and Gerbil was the gerbil.

Life was sweet for them. The beaver dam was warm and dry. The river was full of fish and fun. Hamster and Gerbil got along about 50 percent of the time, which is average for brothers and sisters, adopted or otherwise.

One day when Mama Beaver was on her way home with the week's shopping, a sudden storm came up. A bolt of lightning fell from the sky and struck the trunk of an old pine tree.

Down came the tree. Down came Mama Beaver.

All the forest animals attended the funeral, weeping into the oak leaves that they brought as handkerchiefs. It was awfully sad. It rained during the service and during the sad, wet reception that followed. It was still raining when the grieving family headed home.

But their home was gone, too. The storm had caused the river to overflow its banks. Their beaver dam had been swept away, and the family now had no place to live.

After some looking around, Papa Beaver found a small, damp hole in the side of the riverbank. It was full of worms and spiders, and Hamster and Gerbil didn't like it at all.

"It feels creepy," said Hamster. "It feels haunted."

"It is smelly," said Gerbil. "Frankly, it stinks."

"You're just sad because you miss your mother," said Papa Beaver. "I feel sad too."

They huddled against one another to keep warm. There was nothing to eat because all the fish had been swept down the river out to sea. The sun went down. Against the damp walls, the last weak rays of light slanted. Things could hardly get worse.

Suddenly they did.

"Who's this trespassing in my cave?" said a raw, fierce voice.

The beaver family looked up and trembled. The shape of a forest animal was silhouetted in the door of the cave. They were trapped.

"Papa, I'm scared," murmured Hamster.

"Papa, I can't breathe," mumbled Gerbil. "The walls are closing in on me!"

"Courage, children," said their father. In a louder voice he said, "I'm so sorry, we didn't know this cave was occupied. If you'll move aside, we'll go quietly."

"Papa, I can't breathe either," whispered Hamster. "The air in here smells like the dirty socks of human men."

"Papa, I can't grab my breath," warbled Gerbil, who tended to be dramatic. "The lights are going out! The cruel world is fading away! It reeks of rotten diapers in here!"

"Please," said their father to the imposing shape in the doorway. "Please let us go!"

"Not so fast," said the voice. The shape shifted in the dusk, and a wind came in past the animal. Papa Beaver and Hamster and Gerbil all passed out. The aroma was more or less disgusting.

When Hamster and Gerbil came to their senses, their father said, "Children, I'd like you to meet your new mother. I hope you like her. She's a real skunk. Her name is Skunk."

She *was* a real skunk, and she smelled like one too.

"She said if I didn't marry her she would squirt us with her extra-strength industrial-action high-tech preemptive-strike joy juice," said Papa Beaver in a defeated voice. "I couldn't do that to you."

"Just what I wanted, a hubby!" said Skunk. "And two annoying little children to boss around. Whoopie. My lucky day."

Warning them not to run away, Skunk went outside and found some skunk cabbage. She brought it back and gave it to them for dinner. "Eat up, for that's all there is," she said. "Don't let anyone say I don't provide for my family."

"I'm not eating this tripe," said Hamster bravely.

"Are you talking to me?" said Skunk. "Are you talking to *me*?"

"I'm not eating it either," remarked Gerbil. "Not to be rude or anything, but quite frankly, this meal *stinks*."

"Can I believe my ears?" screamed Skunk. "Ungrateful children! After all I've done for you! For that, you can go to bed without any supper!" And Skunk fell on the skunk cabbage and ate it, chewing with her mouth open, which made the children even more grossed out than ever.

They crawled off to bed. Papa Beaver lowered himself next to them, letting his children sleep behind his back. Trying to breathe through their mouths so as to avoid inhaling stench, Hamster and Gerbil cried themselves to sleep.

Hamster woke up in the middle of the night because his stomach was rumbling with hunger pains. He heard his father and his new stepmother talking.

"Please don't be cruel to them," said Papa Beaver. "They've already had a hard life."

"If you can't provide for them, then neither can I," said Skunk. "I think I'll wake them up and take them out for a walk in the woods and lose them."

"Oh, don't do that," cried Papa Beaver.

"Try and stop me," said the Skunk. "If I lift my tail, you won't know what hit you."

"I forbid it!" cried Papa Beaver. "Over my dead body!"

"Your funeral," said Skunk. She gave him a little zap, and Papa Beaver keeled over with his four legs straight up in the air like a table turned upside down. "Now I'm cooking with gas," said Skunk proudly, and she kicked Gerbil to wake her up. "Yo. Gerbil. Hamster. We're going for a little nature walk. Papa's sound asleep so come quietly."

"Do as she says," whispered Hamster to his sister, "because you have asthma, and if she squirts you, you'll be a goner." Even though his father seemed to be in a coma, Hamster could see that he was still breathing. So it seemed safest just to do as they were told.

Skunk wandered into the forest. Hamster and Gerbil

followed her. When they were far away from anyplace Hamster and Gerbil had ever seen, Skunk said, "Oh, I think I smell a rat over there. Let me go kill it and bring it to you for a little midnight snack. Wait here." And off she went.

"How she can smell anything besides herself is hard to understand," said Gerbil, and she wept softly, and Hamster wept too.

But Skunk disappeared. When the hours passed and she didn't come back, it became clear that their step-mother had abandoned them to die all alone.

Clouds cloaked the moon so they couldn't find their way home. And the woods were alive with the sounds of hooting owls and the rustling of snakes. "Hamster, I'm scared," said Gerbil.

"Sissy," said Hamster. "I'm not."

They began to wander, looking for some food. The only things they could find growing on the forest floor were poison mushrooms. "Hamster, I'm hungry," said Gerbil.

"That happens when you don't eat," he explained.

She bit him on the tail to show that she already knew that.

He bit her on the tail to show her that he knew that she knew.

They bit each other on the tails for quite a while and chased each other through the woods. Out of awful hunger they might have eaten each other right down to the bone, which wouldn't have been a very brotherly or sisterly thing to do. But just when things got a little too ouchy, they stumbled out of the woods into a clearing.

The clouds obligingly parted to let in the light of the moon. Hamster and Gerbil both saw something that made them say, "Wow! Awesome!"

In front of them was a little house made out of pet food.

The house had walls made out of dog biscuits. Cunning little paths around it were strewn with hamster and gerbil food. The roof was made of a scrumptious fresh lettuce leaf, and the chimney was made of a big hollow steak bone. Out of the chimney came the delicious smell of hot stewing kitty friskies, in flavors of chicken, liver, and fish.

"Oh Hamster," cried Gerbil, "is this heaven?"

"I think it's a dream," said Hamster. "But let's go test it with our teeth."

With joy and hunger they fell upon the house. Hamster began to nibble up the front walk. Gerbil climbed on the windowsill and munched on the edge of the roof. It was almost too delicious to be true.

A slug on the lettuce leaf above woke up and said in a bored voice, "My goodness, Granny Porky, look who's here nibbling you out of house and home."

The door flew open. Out stepped the hugest old porcupine that Hamster and Gerbil had ever seen.

"Nibble nibble on my house, are you just a little mouse?" she cried. She was pretty shortsighted, and she'd left her glasses on the butcher-block table inside.

"No, I'm a hamster," said Hamster. "Name of Hamster."

She had caught him by the tail. "A skinny little thing," she said. "You want fattening up."

"Don't forget the munching on the roof, Granny Porky," droned the slug.

Granny Porky reached up and gripped Gerbil's tail. "Nibble nibble on my house, are you just a little mouse?" she said again.

"I'm a gerbil, and proud of it!" cried Gerbil.

"You're a trespasser and I ought to charge you with assault and peppery," said Granny Porky. "But then

again, I need a maid. My eyes are going. I can't read the cookbooks anymore. I can't open the spice jars. You can be my sous chef and I'll drop the charges. What's your name?"

"Gerbil," said Gerbil. "Will you feed us if I work for you?"

"They don't call me Granny Porky for nothing," said the porcupine. She hustled the brother and sister into her house. It smelled even more delicious inside than outside. Bread was baking in the oven, garlic was sizzling in butter on the range, and a pile of fresh basil leaves were heaped redolently on a cutting board.

They had little time to take in the well-planned gourmet kitchen. With a strength surprising in one so old and feeble, Granny Porky lifted Hamster by the scruff of the neck. She tossed him into a cage shaped like a metal hamster wheel that she happened to have in the corner of the room. With a key that she kept on a string around her neck, she locked the door.

"Now, dearie," she said to Gerbil, "do what I tell you when I tell you to do it, and you and your brother will have plenty to eat."

"I would rather not be locked in this hamster wheel," said Hamster.

"Run," said Granny Porky. "I like a hamster with a good rump on it. You have to build up those muscles if you're going to be of use to me." She gave the wheel a turn. "It's the wheel of fortune! Ha-ha-ha!"

"That's not funny," said Gerbil.

"I'll show you funny," said Granny Porky, and she shot out a quill. It pinned Gerbil against the wall like an arrow. "Now are you going to be my slave, or do I have gerbil giblets for supper?"

"At your beck and call, my queen," said Gerbil in a small voice.

"The thing is," said Granny Porky, releasing the quill, "I want to have a big party. The do of the season.

All the creepiest creatures of the woods will be coming. Owls and spiders and snakes and rats and vampire bats and the like. I need to serve a very special meal. I've been combing through my back issues of *Gourmet* magazine. I thought maybe a platter of hamster chops. What do you think?"

"Yuck," said Gerbil.

"Yikes!" said Hamster, and ran faster, but he couldn't get away because hamster wheels just turn around and around in one place. And he couldn't knock it over because the pin around which the wheel rotated was hammered into the wall.

"You may begin by scrubbing last night's dishes," said Granny Porky to Gerbil, and she pointed to a heap of high-quality copper pans and ceramic baking dishes, all encrusted with the kind of cheesy-eggy mixture that never comes off.

Granny Porky slumped into a rocker and fell asleep by the hearth. Gerbil put some wooden spoons to soak for a minute, and then she ran over to her brother.

"I'll save you," she said. "Be brave."

"How?" he said.

"I don't know," she said. "I'll think of something."

"Do," he said, "if you don't mind." And he ran as fast as he could, tears streaming out of his eyes and pooling up on the floor.

For a whole week Hamster ran. Every once in a while Granny Porky would come by and stop the wheel with her gnarled old paw, and she reached in to feel Hamster's thighs to see if he was ready for butchering yet. But Gerbil had given Hamster a straw from the broom, and he held this forward when Granny Porky asked to feel his arm. "You're thinner than ever!" Granny Porky roared. "With all I feed you? I don't get it!"

One day the slug had chewed up so much of the roof that he fell through onto the sofa. In a lazy voice he said, "Granny Porky, that's a broom straw you're testing for meat. You'd better get yourself some new glasses."

"Why, you little hamster," screamed the porcupine. "I'll roast you up tonight for that! Gerbil, build up the fire! We're going to have shake-and-bake hamster cutlets!"

"No!" screamed Gerbil.

"How about Hamster Helper?" asked the porcupine, drooling at the thought.

"Gross!" said Gerbil.

"Little cocktail snacks, then," said the porcupine decisively. "If I blow out all my quills, we could use them for toothpicks. We could put a chunk of Hamster, a chunk of pineapple, a chunk of Hamster, a chunk of onion, and round it off with a cherry tomato. What do you think?"

"You make me sick to my stomach," said Gerbil.

"At least you still have a stomach," said Hamster, and cried all the harder.

But Granny Porky was decided. She blew out all her quills and put them in a pile on the floor. Then she opened up a can of pineapple chunks. She made Gerbil stoke the fire in the oven until it was five hundred degrees. All the while she sang to herself. "Oh my darling, oh my darling, oh my darling porcupine," she crooned. "Little critters fried like fritters come out crunchy and divine."

"Watch the gerbil," said the slug. "She's smarter than she looks."

"Shouldn't you send the slug off to invite the guests?" said Gerbil.

"Good idea," said Granny Porky. "Slug, make tracks."

The slug crawled away, sighing.

Granny Porky poked all her quills into a pincushion for easy handling. Then she washed some cherry tomatoes. "All we need is the meat," she said. "Gerbil, my dear, would you crawl into the oven and see if it's hot enough?"

Gerbil went over to the oven and opened the door. "I can't tell, Granny Porky," she said.

"What do you mean, you can't tell?" said Granny Porky. "You dolt. Feel it with your hand."

"My hand is too tired from housework to feel heat anymore," said Gerbil.

"Well, for the love of nothing," snapped Granny Porky. "Do I have to do everything?"

"Beware that smart little gerbil," called the slug from the front walk. He couldn't move very fast and he was watching through the door. Gerbil ran over and slammed the door shut.

"Show me how to tell if it's hot enough," said Gerbil.

"Just climb inside," said Granny Porky nastily. She thought she could fling the oven door closed and have juicy gerbil legs for her party, too.

"I can't climb," said Gerbil. "My limbs are aching from all the housework. I have a pinched nerve in my spine."

"You simpleton," snapped Granny Porky. "It isn't hard! Just lean over and crawl in!"

"Show me," said Gerbil.

"Beware," called the slug, but Hamster started singing the national anthem just then to drown out the slug's warning. Granny Porky hobbled across the kitchen floor, naked of all her bristles and wearing nothing but a filthy old apron. She climbed into the oven and said, "See, you foolish animal, now do you see what I mean?"

"Now I see what you mean, you old beast," shouted Gerbil, and she slammed the oven door shut and locked it.

And that was the end of Granny Porky. Except for her quills.

Unfortunately, the key to the hamster wheel had burned up and melted down inside the oven, and Gerbil didn't know how to open the cage. But after three days of chewing, she managed at least to break the wheel free from the wall. Then she opened the door and gave the wheel a push.

Hamster raced the cage proudly out the door and down the path. With a glorious crunch, he ran over the slug, who in three whole days of traveling had only made it to the bottom of the garden.

Gerbil took up Granny Porky's pincushion—very gently, very carefully. She also helped herself to several of the better cookbooks, the reading of which she had grown fond.

With Hamster rolling in his wheel beside her, they set off through the woods. After many mishaps and wrong turns, they finally made it back to the riverbank where they had last seen their father.

And there he was! He hadn't died of the stink attack! However, Skunk had fed him on nothing but bits of predigested skunk cabbage, and he'd lost a lot of weight. So he wasn't looking his best.

But he was so delighted to see his children again that he felt better at once. With his strong beaver teeth he gnawed through the lock of the hamster cage.

Then Hamster and Gerbil told him how Skunk had tried to lose them in the forest, hoping they would starve to death. "She's an evil thing," said Papa Beaver. "The world would be better rid of her."

So they devised a plan. They found some choice bits of skunk cabbage and marinated it in a paste made of mold, mildew, and mayonnaise. They worked on it in secret, and when it was ready, they rolled it like a ball, like a special cocktail snack, and put it in the hamster wheel. Then they rolled the hamster wheel onto the top of the bluff overlooking the river.

When it was all ready, Hamster and Gerbil hid behind a clump of dandelions. "Oh darling," Papa Beaver called, "I've made you a special treat."

"It better be good, you worthless lump of beaver!" screamed Skunk, coming out of the cave. "I don't know why I ever bothered to marry you anyway! You've been nothing but trouble since the moment we met! Marry in haste, repent in leisure! At least those annoying little kids of yours are dead! That's the only fun I ever got out of this marriage!"

"I put your food in that private little dining room," said Papa Beaver. "That way no one else will steal it."

"Now you're thinking," said Skunk. "This meal stinks to high heaven. You're finally learning to cook the way I like it."

"I hope you like *this*," said Papa Beaver.

Skunk climbed into the hamster wheel. It was a tight fit, but she settled down to nibble at her meal. When her back was turned, Papa Beaver slammed the door of the hamster wheel behind her.

"What did you do that for, you buck-toothed bozo?" yelled Skunk.

"A little more privacy," said Papa Beaver.

She ate a little more. Suddenly she began to scream. Her mouth was filled with porcupine quills, because the smelly food was wrapped around the pincushion bristly with Granny Porky's spikes.

"Doctor! Dentist! Yowza-dowza!" she wailed. "Will no one help me?"

Just then Hamster and Gerbil scampered up and gave the hamster wheel a little push.

"You are still alive! You twerps!" cried Skunk. She tried to hose them with her worst chemical-weapon spray, but her aim was poor. Her tail was curled around herself, and she ended up spritzing herself.

The hamster wheel picked up speed and pitched over the bluff into the river. Skunk was never seen again, but a cloud of skunk-smog hung over the river-bank for a month.

Papa Beaver and his beloved children began imme-diately to build themselves a new beaver dam. Even

though they still missed Mama Beaver, they were happy being back together. And when Papa Beaver eventually fell in love with a cute vixen from across the valley, Hamster and Gerbil liked her quite a bit too.

They got together and combed through the cookbooks and settled on some fancy items to prepare for the wedding feast. At first they were sorely tempted to try a huge roast of porcupine, but that seemed a bit too mean, even under the circumstances. They settled on a board of very fancy stinky cheeses. The aroma made everyone think of Skunk, and how nice it was that she had floated far away.

SO WHAT
AND THE
SEVEN GIRAFFES

One day the king of the baboons said, "I want a child."

"And how does that make you feel?" asked the queen.

"I am so sad," said the king.

"I feel your pain," said the queen.

"Thank you for caring," said the king.

"Thank you for sharing," said the queen.

Yes, the king and queen were sad, and they heard what each other was saying, and they knew where each other was coming from. They had a perfect marriage, in fact. When the queen filled out a questionnaire called "How Is Your Marriage?" in the back of *Baboons' Home Journal*, her score was great. Her marriage was healthy. It was in such perfect health that she wrote a letter to the editor to ask, "So why am I not pregnant?"

"Sew yourself a little cross-stitch motto," the editor wrote back. "If you prick your finger on the needle and the blood comes out, make a wish."

The queen didn't care much for sewing. But dutifully she got a needle and thread and began to stitch a motto on a piece of cloth. She was going to make a little sign saying BABY ON BOARD and wear it like an apron if she got pregnant. Then she pricked her thumb and a drop of blood came out. "I wish I could have a baby," she cried. "I wish my thumb didn't hurt so much! I hope I don't get blood poisoning! Just because I have to sew this thing!"

"Sew what?" said the king, coming in.

She showed him the sampler, but all it said so far was BABY.

A couple of weeks later, the queen realized that she was pregnant.

"You look radiant," said the king fondly.

"I have got a whoopsy tummy," said the queen, and proved it.

"I feel your pain," said the king.

"That's what *you* think," said the queen. "Can you get blood poisoning from a needle?"

"Maybe," said the king. "I'm here for you. Let me share."

"I would if I could," said the queen. "My blue behind, can this monster in here kick or what?"

"Try being sweet and understanding to it," said the king.

The queen put her hand on her swelling stomach and patted it. "I'm there for you," she said to the baby inside.

From inside, the baby kicked so hard that the queen got a lump on her palm the size of a meatball.

The king put his ear to the queen's stomach. "I'll spend a little quality time with my child," he said. "Hi there, child of mine. I hear where you're coming from." Inside the queen the baby began to screech and fuss so loudly that the king went almost completely deaf. "How can you stand that noise, my dear?" he asked his wife.

71

But his wife didn't hear what he was saying because she had put earplugs in her ears.

Finally the queen gave birth to a cunning little boy chimpanzee. The chimp wriggled in her arms like a wrinkling piece of bacon. "I love you," said the queen fondly.

"So what?" said the chimp.

The queen took her earplugs out. "Did I see your lips move? Can you talk? King, come listen to this!"

But the king didn't hear her. He was in the royal garage, busy making a hearing trumpet out of a conch shell.

The queen didn't feel so hot. "I hoped and prayed for you my whole life long," she murmured to her baby. "I'm so thrilled you're here."

"So what?" said the chimp.

The queen was so surprised that her newborn baby could talk that she died of happiness. Or maybe it was shock. Or blood poisoning.

The king mourned and vowed to raise his son in the

paths of niceness. But everybody called the chimp by the name of So What, because that was the main thing that he said.

So What was a little devil. He jumped on his father's hearing trumpets and smashed them. So his father the king wandered around in a constant state of baboon deafness. He couldn't hear how rude his son was. He loved his son.

Eventually the king got married again, this time to a body-building gorilla from the suburbs. The new queen was fond of So What for about two minutes. Then she got over it.

"You and I are going to get along or I'll break your little neck," she told him.

"So what?" said So What.

"So then you'll have to wear a neck brace like a huge peppermint LifeSaver."

"So what?"

"Say another word, So What, and so help me . . ."

"So help you what?" he said.

The gorilla queen threw a lamp across the room. She didn't throw it at So What. She just threw it to release a little nervous energy. So What scampered away, laughing wickedly.

In the days to come So What delighted in goading his stepmother into throwing lamps. She became quite good at it. Soon, if she got a decent head of steam up, she could heave a standing floor lamp a distance of a hundred fifty feet.

But So What got on her nerves, and the king was lost in a fog of permanent deafness. He was constantly tooling conch shells into new hearing aids that So What stomped on. Between the smashing of lamps and the stomping on conch shells, it was one noisy castle.

Finally the gorilla queen had had enough. She wrote a letter to the editor of *Baboons' Home Journal* and asked for advice. The editor printed her letter (but in order to protect her privacy, changed her name from "Gorilla Queen" to "Worried in the Royal Castle"). The editor

suggested hiring a local hunter to take the little trou-
blemaker out into the woods, kill him, and cut his heart
out and bring it back. "Check page 44 of last month's
issue for delicious recipes, at just pennies a serving!" she
concluded.

The gorilla hired a hunter. He was a human being.
Humans are good at hunting. But when the human
being got So What to the clearing in the forest, So What
fell to his knees and begged for forgiveness. "Please
don't kill me," he cried. "I can't help being nasty. It's the
way I am."

"Everyone can help how they are," said the hunter
firmly. But some humans are good at kindness as well
as hunting. This hunter was one of those. He took pity
on the little chimp and said, "Run for your life, So
What, for that gorilla stepmother of yours doesn't put
up with any nonsense. If she finds I haven't killed you,
she'll come after you and throw a lamp at you or something. One of these days the lamp will still be plugged
in and you'll get electrocuted. Run, run, I say, and I'll

buy a piece of chicken liver in the supermarket on the way home and tell her it's your heart."

"You would do that for me?" said So What.

"Humans are good at lying," said the hunter. "Besides, a chicken liver is a tiny thing, and that's about how big your heart is so far. I hope you learn some manners, my boy. If you were my chimp, I'd put you over my knee and give you a good spanking."

"So what," said the chimp.

"So long," said the hunter, and he made good his promise. When the queen saw the chicken liver lying in a little Styrofoam carton, she cooked it up with onions and sherry and ate it for a snack. Then she went to tell her husband that their little boy seemed to have run away. The king got a flashlight and went to hunt in the hedges, but he couldn't find his boy.

Meanwhile, So What wandered in the forest looking for someone to annoy. He considered throwing stones at squirrels, or throwing squirrels at stones, but he could only find stones. It was too dark and gloomy in the forest for right-thinking squirrels.

So What wasn't used to being on his own and he became bored with no one to pester. But just before night fell, he wandered into a clearing in the middle of the big woods. There he saw the strangest house. It had a roof of straw and beautiful diamond-paned windows that badly wanted cleaning with a solution of water and ammonia. It had an overgrown flower garden in the front. And the whole thing was about as tall as a high school gymnasium.

"Welcome to the Land of the Giants," whispered So What to himself, and because he was curious and hungry, he crept closer.

He opened the door, which was tall enough to carry a Christmas tree through without clipping the top branches.

Inside, So What found a terrible mess. There were seven hooks high on the wall—much too high for him to reach, as he was only a little chimp. There was a table with seven enormously tall chairs, almost like seven stepladders. In another corner of the room there were seven long beds beside each other; they looked like seven lanes in a bowling alley. Except they were not made.

"What a mess!" said So What. "Whoever lives here is a bunch of slobs!"

So What looked for something to eat. The icebox was filled with about a hundred heads of lettuce. Then, because he was so bored, he began to trash the place. But since it was such a mess already, he couldn't make it much worse. It wasn't much fun.

After a while he grew tired, and he fell asleep at the foot of one of the seven beds.

He didn't hear the noise of hooves tripping through the forest when evening came. But before long the door opened, and the owners of the tall house in the big woods came home.

They were seven giraffes who worked at a nearby circus. Their names were Pumpkin, Goldskin, Jackie-lantern, Orangelight, Nimble, Limber, and Kimberly.

"Someone has been trashing our house," said Goldskin.

"Who would bother?" said Nimble.

"Someone has been thrashing and mashing our lettuces," said Pumpkin.

"Who would care?" said Limber.

"Someone has been jumping on our sofa," said Orangelight.

"Someone has been thumping through our garden," said Jackielantern.

"Someone has been rumpling up the blankets on my bed, and here he is!" said Kimberly. "Isn't he an ugly little thing!"

Just then So What woke up to find the seven giraffes looking over him. They were still dressed in their work clothes: spangles, capes, tights, and caps with brightly colored ostrich feathers.

So What had never been to the circus, and he had never seen giraffes before. He screamed like a psycho chimp.

"Someone has a powerful set of lungs," said Kimberly.

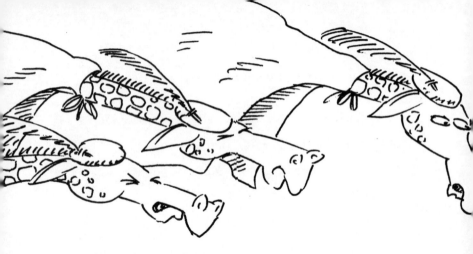

"There, there, my dear. What brings you to our tall home
in the forest?"

When So What calmed down, he told them that his
wicked stepmother had wanted to cut his heart out and
eat it.

"That reminds me, what are *we* having for supper?" said Goldskin.

"Lettuce," said her six sisters.

"This is a horror story," said Jackielantern to So What.

"We giraffes will pro-tect you. Would you like to stay with us and be our houseboy? We need some help. We work too hard to do housework at the end of a long day, and besides, we hate it. Life Is Too Short to Vacuum Every Day! That's my motto."

"Work? Me work?" said So What. "Lady, you're out of your gourd."

"It's either work or walk," said Jackielantern. "We'll protect you if you keep our home as neat as a pin. If you don't like the deal, find yourself somewhere else to hole up. We're not the Witness Protection Bureau. Sisters, am I right? Back me up here!"

The other giraffes agreed, and therefore So What was allowed to stay on in the tall house. Though he griped and whined about it, he learned how to do housework when the giraffe sisters were out at work in the circus every day. He got pretty good at folding crisp hospital corners in the bedsheets and keeping the very tall toilet spotlessly clean, with the help of a toilet scrubber the size of a floor lamp.

So What begged to be allowed to come along, but the giraffes always said, "What if your gorilla stepmother comes to the circus one day and sees you there? That would be the end of you. No, my boy, stay home and polish the silver. And weed the vegetables. And clean the windows. And vacuum. And so on."

Though he still talked big, So What found he was glad he hadn't been killed by a hunter and his heart served up as an hors d'oeuvre. He really rather liked being alive. From a mail-order catalog, So What bought a pair of stilts so he could hang up the giraffes' circus clothes when they came home and flopped into bed, one after the other, like a whole stand of pine trees being felled by a chain saw.

Back at the castle, the king could hear better now that no one was around to stomp on his ear trumpets. He began to listen to what his new wife was saying, and he realized that he had made a mistake choosing her for a wife. But she had developed such a powerful arm with that lamp-throwing business that he was afraid to cross her. So he stayed in his throne room most of the day, reading the paper.

The gorilla queen bought a full-length mirror at a garage sale. Every morning after breakfast she went to her boudoir and gazed at herself. She practiced making muscles. One day, making "I'm the champion!" victory signs at herself, she said,

> *"Mirror mirror on the wall,*
> *Who's the strongest of them all?"*

To her surprise, the mirror spoke back to her. It said,

> *"Gorilla Queen, Gorilla Queen,*
> *You're the strongest I've ever seen."*

"Well, fancy that, a chatty mirror," said the gorilla. "And one that tells the truth, too. Thank you, mirror." Then she kissed the mirror, but she was really kissing herself.

One day, however, the gorilla said,

> *"Mirror mirror on the wall,*
> *Who's the strongest of them all?"*

This time the mirror answered,

> *"Gorilla Queen, you preen and strut.*
> *You're not the strongest, though. So what?"*

"So What!" seethed the gorilla. "Do you mean that little twerp is still alive?"

> *"Unless you talk in simple rhyme,*
> *You're simply wasting both our time,"*

said the mirror.

The gorilla queen clenched her teeth and tried again:

> *"Where does he live? Is he near? Is he far?*
> *Tell me, you stupid flat-faced mirror!"*

The mirror thought for a bit. *Far* and *mirror* aren't really rhymes, and the scansion was dicey. But at the expression of the gorilla, the mirror decided to let it pass. It replied,

"In a house with seven lady giraffes,
He is the houseboy. How's that for laughs!"

The gorilla queen lost no time in firing the hunter who had given her the chicken liver. He found another job as the ringmaster at the same circus the giraffes worked for.

The gorilla queen looked up the giraffes' address in the phone book. Then she sat down and thought how she could kill So What. *She* wanted to be the strongest of them all. Down into her exercise dungeon she went and did a hundred push-ups for inspiration.

Finally she had an idea. She could poison him! If he was so strong, he must be a mighty eater.

She raced to the market and bought a bunch of bananas, and then she barreled into the library and looked up how to poison them.

It was but the work of an afternoon to coat the banana with a very special yellow poison that looked just like the skin of a banana. The fact that it smelled like a slice of toxic salami was a bit worrying. But the gorilla queen disguised herself as a Merry Maid of the Forest and sprayed on eight ounces of Jungle Spirit, a new cologne she'd read about in *Baboons' Home Journal*. She went bounding like a triathlete through the forest, carrying a basket of bananas with her.

When she found the tall house in the forest, she pounded on the door until So What came to see what the racket was. He was still a little chimp. He didn't look so very strong. But she couldn't take any chances.

"Pardon me, kind sir. I'm selling fresh bananas," she said in her sweetest voice.

"So what?" said So What.

"Would you like to buy one?"

"No," said So What, "I'm in training. I hope to get a job in the circus someday, so I'm doing my housework as fast as I can and working out for the rest of the day. Besides, I don't have any money."

"This one doesn't cost anything," said the gorilla

queen. She threw the poison banana at him with the deadly accuracy for which she was so well known. It slid right down So What's throat. "Yum," said So What, making a face at the smell, and he fell over on the floor.

When the seven giraffes came back that evening, they found So What in a dead faint. Jackielantern called the trauma center, and over the phone the nurse explained how to do the Heimlich maneuver.

Orangelight held So What's arms, and Limber held his legs, and the others counted to three, and Kimberly crossed her delicate legs across So What's chest and pulled with all her might. The lump of poison banana shot out.

"Yuck," said the giraffes.

"I'm alive again!" cried So What.

"When you're feeling a little better, clean up that mess," said Pumpkin. "That's what comes of snacking between meals."

"But this banana was poisoned!" cried Nimble, who was sniffing at the banana with her nimble nose. "Where did you get it?"

So What explained about the Merry Maid of the Forest selling bananas.

"This sounds suspicious to me," said Goldskin.

"Better not answer the door again unless one of us is here to protect you," said Kimberly. "You may be getting stronger, So What, but you're still young and immature and a little stupid. Though in a pleasant way," she added, when she saw how hurt he looked.

The next day the gorilla queen spoke to her mirror again. She said,

> *"Mirror mirror on the wall,*
> *Who's the strongest of them all?"*

The mirror answered,

> *"Your mighty arms and chest and butt*
> *Are not the strongest now. So what?"*

"That little creep is a disaster area waiting to be declared!" cried the gorilla queen. She flipped through old volumes of *Baboons' Home Journal* and looked for sewing patterns. She found a design for a pair of fancy silk athletic shorts. She wasn't much for sewing, but she bought some material and a needle the size of a hypodermic and stitched together a dazzling pair of athletic trunks with silver sequins and a peekaboo slit on the left thigh. Then she dressed herself up as a Dizzy Dame of the Forest and went sprinting through the woods.

When she got to the tall house in the clearing, she hammered on the door and said, "Attention inside! You may have won this smart pair of athletic shorts! Would you like to answer one simple question and see if you've won?"

"No," cried So What through the window.

"That's the correct answer! You've won first prize!" cried the gorilla queen. "Open up the door and try these on for size, big boy!"

So What knew he shouldn't open the door, but the snazzy shorts looked so terrific that he couldn't help himself. He came outside and admired the fine needlework on the shorts. "If my friends ever take me to the circus, I could wear these when I'm shot from the cannon!" he said. "It sort of turns my stomach to talk to someone as hideous as you, but may I try them on?"

"They're yours; do what you like," said the gorilla queen.

So What took off his apron and his yellow plastic gloves and dropped the toilet bowl brush with which he'd been scrubbing. He put on the shorts. They looked swell. "Here, let me tie them for you," said the gorilla queen, and she reached for the strings around the waistband. "Breathe in."

So What breathed in, but not enough. The gorilla queen yanked those strings so hard that his breath left him entirely, and he fell down in a dead faint. Then the gorilla queen tied the strings in a double trouble sailor-boy knot and sealed it with glue and sealing wax and a small bit of quick-drying cement she carried in her purse, so the knot wouldn't come undone. Then she vaulted away, cackling like a witch.

When the giraffes came home, they saw So What by the front door. He was nearly gray with lack of air.

The seven giraffes had strong teeth from all that lettuce nibbling. Besides, Pumpkin and Goldskin were excellent trapeze artists and, daily, hung from a rope by their teeth at the highest point of the big top. So all seven of them set to work on the waistband.

Finally they had nibbled it through, and the waistband relaxed. So What breathed in such a big breath that all the furniture inside the house came rushing from the suction and got stuck in a clot in the doorway.

When he could speak again, he said, "Aren't these the best shorts you ever saw?"

"They need a new waistband," said Nimble. "Where did you get them, So What?"

"From a pretty sorry-looking Dizzy Dame of the Forest," said So What, but he bowed his head in shame when they told him he had almost been murdered once more.

"You misbehaved again," said Orangelight. "Do you know how we would feel if we lost you, dear boy?"

"So what," he muttered, but really he felt terrible. "I wouldn't be doing this if you'd let me come to the circus with you!" he cried. "I'm sick of all the housework!"

"No, the wicked gorilla queen might see you there," said the giraffes. "It's too risky. You must stay home and you must stay inside until you grow even stronger and better able to take care of yourself. You're a good strong chimp, but are you any match for a gorilla? We think not. Behave yourself, now."

The next morning the gorilla queen said to her mirror,

> *"Mirror mirror on the wall,*
> *Who's the strongest one of all?*
> *You're lying if you name that chimp.*
> *Compared to me, he's a wilting wimp."*

93

The mirror said,

> *"Why do you want eternal youth?*
> *Why shouldn't furniture tell the truth?*
> *Queen, you're stuck in a dismal rut.*
> *Who cares who's strongest now? So what?"*

The queen was so furious that she threw a floor lamp at the mirror and broke it into a million pieces. It never offered another opinion again.

Then the queen had an idea. She got some handcuffs and a blindfold and some rope and she dressed herself like a policewoman and went swinging through the jungle. When she got to the tall house in the big woods, she let herself slam against the front door and she cried out in a huge and horrible voice, "This is the police! We have you surrounded. Open up!"

But nobody came to the door.

"The police don't take no for an answer! At the count of three, we're coming in!"

Still no answer.

"One two three," she roared, and smashed the door down.

But no one was home. There was a note on the kitchen table.

Dear Friends,

I couldn't stand worrying you any more, so I went to the circus disguised as the Cannonball Chimp. That was me you sent shooting through the roof of the tent! I've moved on. It was nice knowing you.

So What

The gorilla raced as fast as she could go to the circus. When she got there, she didn't have enough money for a ticket. So she arrested the ticket seller and locked him up in handcuffs. Then she rushed into the tent anyway.

Inside, the giraffes were just finishing their acrobatics. Limber and Nimble were riding unicycles on the high wire. Orangelight and Jackielantern were swaying on the flying trapeze, tossing Kimberly back and forth between them. Pumpkin and Goldskin were getting the cannon ready for the finale.

"And now, ladies and gentlemen!" cried the ringmaster, who as you remember was the hunter whom the gorilla queen had fired. "For your delight and terror! A feat never before attempted in circus history! Our new star, the Cannonball Chimp, is going to be shot out of the cannon, between the jaws of a lion, over the tank of piranhas, and through the hoop of fire! All without a safety net! All without life insurance! Sit back, hush, and prepare to be amazed! The Cannonball Chimp is the strongest one of all!"

Pumpkin and Goldskin helped the Cannonball Chimp into the cannon. They should have recognized him, for he was wearing his silvery athletic shorts repaired with a safety pin. But they were too hard at work to notice the similarity between him and their houseboy.

"On your mark!" called the ringmaster, lighting the fuse.

"Stop!" cried the gorilla queen. "That Cannonball Chimp is under arrest!"

"The show must go on!" answered the ringmaster. "Get set!"

"It's the gorilla queen!" yelled Kimberly. "She's after the Cannonball Chimp! It must be—"

"SO WHAT!" the other giraffes cried.

"GO!" shouted the ringmaster.

The cannon fired. So What shot out so fast that his silvery athletic shorts came off, and the lion ate them.

So What zipped over the piranhas, whose mouths were watering. He zoomed through the hoop of fire, whose flames licked at him. But he went so fast and so high that it looked as if he was going to rip a hole right through the tent and keep on going.

"Oh no, you don't!" screamed the gorilla queen. She picked up a chair used for taunting the lion. She hurled it through the air.

It wasn't a floor lamp, but it did the trick. It intercepted So What and clobbered him on the noggin.

He fell with a splash into the tank of piranhas. They would have eaten him up if they hadn't been all washed out in the huge wave that drenched the gorilla queen in her policewoman's costume. They ate her up instead.

But So What was out cold, and it seemed that he was dead.

The seven giraffes knelt around the chimp and tried everything. But nothing would work. Weeping salty tears of grief, they carried him home to their tall house

in the big woods. There they set So What in a coffin under a banana tree, and one of them kept watch over him by night and day while the other six performed in the circus.

"Even though you used to get our toothbrushes mixed up, I miss you," said Pumpkin.

"Even though you left the lettuce out in the rain to wilt, I miss you," said Orangelight.

"Even though you broke the springs on my bed by jumping on it, I miss you," said Nimble.

"Even though you put itching powder in my sky blue sequinned tights, I miss you," said Limber.

"Even though you glued my feet together while I was asleep, I miss you," said Goldskin.

"Even though you broke the vacuum cleaner by trying to suck up the backyard with it, I miss you," said Kimberly.

"I don't miss you at all. So you're dead. So what?" said Jackielantern. But everyone knew she was just saying that.

As the years went by, many princesses of different varieties came by the coffin. They looked in the glass lid. Whoever was on duty that day would say, "Would you like to give our little houseboy a kiss? He's been dead a long time."

But the princesses always answered, "So what?" and went on their way.

Finally one gloomy evening an old baboon with a hearing trumpet came by. It was the former king. He had retired from his job and spent his golden years mourning for his first wife and his long-dead son. When he came into the clearing, he wandered nearer to say hello to the seven giraffes. Because the evening was pleasant, they were having a picnic. They had spread a checkered tablecloth over the glass lid of the coffin. On top of the cloth they had put their plastic picnic plates piled high with lettuce.

"Would you like a bite to eat, old baboon?" they asked.

"Eh?" said the baboon. He put his ear trumpet to his head. "Come again?"

"Food?" they shouted.

"Sorry, can't catch what you're saying. I'm an old baboon," he said.

"Are you hungry?" they screamed at the top of their giraffe lungs. They yelled so loudly that the picnic tablecloth blew off. There was the chimp, lying in a state of calm. He hadn't aged a day.

"What's this?" cried the baboon.

"Our houseboy. He's dead," the giraffes answered.

"I recognize him!" said the baboon. He tore the glass lid off the coffin and reached inside. He pulled the limp body of the chimp toward him and kissed him tenderly. "I love you!" he said.

The chimp opened his eyes. "Papa?" he said.

"It *is* you!" sobbed his father.

"So What," the chimp agreed.

"*That's* what," said his father firmly, and kissed him again. "You're coming home with me, son, and we're going to change your name. I'm so delighted and surprised to have you back with me again, I'm going to call you Slap Me Silly."

"Slap Me Silly," said the chimp. And all the giraffes did.

Slap Me Silly and his father went home. And whenever anyone asked, "What's your name?" the chimp had to answer "Slap Me Silly." And everyone did.

The chimp found he was a lot less inclined to misbehave once everyone had gotten into the habit of slapping him silly at the drop of a hat. He became a good obedient son and remained a whiz at housework, too.

Slap Me Silly also got a new pair of attractive silver shorts. He went to work in the circus with the seven giraffes. Once a year the chimp and his father and the giraffes all took a long vacation together—usually to someplace they had read about in *Baboons' Home Journal.*

LITTLE RED
ROBIN HOOD

There was once a little robin who lived with his mother in a cozy nest on the very top of a telephone pole in the middle of the forest.

The little robin was called Little Red Robin Hood, because he *was* a red robin. Also, when he grew up, he wanted to rob the rich birds of the forest and give their worms to the poor birds of the forest.

Little Red Robin Hood pretended he was a superhero with special superpowers. Sometimes he wore a little red cape with a red hood. It was his superhero costume. It made a nice fluttering noise when he flew, like the sound of baseball cards slapping against a rotating bicycle wheel.

One day Mother Robin got a phone call. It was from Grandma Robin. She lived in a retirement village for old birds on the other side of the forest. She had her own apartment, but she took catered meals in the canteen with the other old birds to save herself the trouble of cooking and washing up.

"What's up, you old darling?" said Mother Robin.

"I'm feeling poorly," said Grandma Robin. "It's the flu, maybe. Could you send that little tyke of yours over with some fresh worm salad or something? The cooking here is not worth discussing. I need some building up."

"Of course," said Mother Robin. "How about I make up a basket of wormy goodies? Little Red Robin Hood can fly them over later on in the day."

"I'll leave the key under the mat," said Grandma Robin, "in case I'm taking a nap or watching my soaps. I don't always hear the apartment doorbell."

"Do you need some medicine?" asked Mother Robin.

"A look at my little grandson will perk me right up," said Grandma Robin. "Can't get enough of him. What a sweetheart he is. And so kind. Always wanting to rob from the rich and give to the poor."

"He had *better* not. Charity is charity, but robbing is robbing," said Mother Robin, crooking the phone receiver under her beak as she began to rummage through the fridge for some worms she'd got on sale the day before. "Someday he's going to get into trouble with all this superhero stuff."

"Maybe he shouldn't come here," said Grandma Robin. "I don't want to be a burden. Never mind me. I'll go droop on my perch and wait for good health to return."

"Don't tire yourself out worrying, old darling," said Mother Robin. "Go sit down and rest your weary wings. He'll be there very soon."

"I'll try not to be dead yet," said Grandma Robin, and hung up.

Little Red Robin Hood loved his grandmother dearly. He was happy to help her out, especially if she had the flu. When Mother Robin had the basket of wormy goodies ready, he put on his red hood and cape and a black mask, too. He looked a little bit like a robin who had flown into a plate-glass window and gotten two black eyes out of it.

"My little superhero," said Mother Robin, and kissed her boy fondly. "Now see if you can carry this little basket."

Little Red Robin Hood tried. It was too heavy.

Mother Robin took out the worm fritters, the worm egg rolls, and the jar of worm-and-walnut sauce. "Try now, dearie," she said.

But it was still too heavy. Little Red Robin Hood could just about get off the floor with it, but he couldn't move backward or forward.

So Mother Robin took out the worm grits, the worm gravy, and the worm-and-orange marmalade.

Little Red Robin Hood could pick *this* up. "Now you're flapping your wings," said Mother Robin proudly. "There's still the worm brandy, the worm casserole, and the wormy cheese. That'll hold the old bird over till next weekend. Now be a good little robin, son, and remember our family rule. Don't fly away from the sight of the telephone wires. The forest is dark and deep, and you never know what you'll find there."

"I know what you'll find there," murmured Little Red Robin Hood. "Evil villains. I'm going to beat them up with my superpowers." But his mother couldn't hear what he was saying because the handle of the basket of goodies was clenched in his beak.

Off through the forest flew Little Red Robin Hood. It was a beautiful day. For a while Little Red Robin Hood flew alongside the telephone wires. He could never get lost if he just followed the phone lines from his nest to Grandma's retirement apartment.

But after a while the basket began to seem very heavy. His mother had forgotten all about an old wormy pound cake tucked under a napkin at the bottom of the basket. It weighed *more* than a pound. Little Red Robin Hood decided to set the basket down and rest for a while.

He perched himself on the handle of the basket and tweeted to keep himself brave. After all, it was much darker down here on the ground, underneath the dense branches of the trees.

Suddenly Little Red Robin Hood heard the voice

of a female chickadee. "Oh help!" cried the chickadee from the shadowy reaches of the thicket. "Oh my! Woe is me!"

"This is a job for a superhero!" said Little Red Robin Hood. "I'll save you!"

He valiantly flew into the thicket. But he could find no blushing chickadee girl. Restlessly he fluttered from twig to twig, but the voice seemed to be farther away. "Oh goodness! What an unlucky day for me! Yikes!" twittered the hapless chickadee.

Little Red Robin Hood didn't want to get lost. But he couldn't leave a poor defenseless chickadee alone in the dark woods. "Keep tweeting. I'll find you!" he called, and plunged deeper into the murky forest.

"Glory be! Is there no one to save me? I'm a goner for sure!" screeched the distant chickadee, a bit hysterically.

"Here I come to save the day!" sang Little Red Robin Hood. With cape flapping, he dove into the deepest shadowy depths of the woods.

There he came upon a cat, who had one great paw

on the wing of a mockingbird.

"Thank heavens!" said the mockingbird to the cat. "Here's something juicier than I am. Eat *him* if you're hungry. Let me go."

"Have either of you seen a little chickadee, desperately in need of a superhero?" screamed Little Red Robin Hood.

The cat winked one eye slowly. The mockingbird sighed, and said in a sultry way—imitating the voice of a chickadee girl—"My hero!"

Little Red Robin Hood was stunned. He hadn't known that mockingbirds could imitate chickadees.

"Why, you dastardly villain!" he cried. "You've made me lose my way in the forest! My mother will kill me! And my poor grandma will be looking for her basket of goodies! She lives all alone in a retirement apartment, and she's left the key for me under the mat! She has the flu! How dare you!"

"I do need saving," the mockingbird pointed out. "This cat intends to eat me."

"Purr," said the cat. "Meow. Yum. Any minute now. I'm just waiting till my stomach wakes up."

In the distance a blast of brass music sounded: *ta-ra, ta-ra*. It made Little Red Robin Hood feel as if he really *were* a superhero. "Unhand that bird, you cat! I mean *cad*!" cried Little Red Robin Hood.

"Never." The cat sighed. "Unless you let me eat you

instead. I'm almost hungry enough."

Little Red Robin Hood didn't think *that* was such a good idea.

"I'll go and look for my basket of goodies, and then I'll come back and drop them on your captor's head," he said to the mockingbird. "There's a whole pound cake in there. It'll hurt like crazy."

"We don't have time for that," said the mockingbird. "Can't you think of something else?"

The trumpet music sounded again, closer this time. It stirred Little Red Robin Hood's blood. He had another idea. "If I fly back to the phone wires," said Little Red Robin Hood, "I can pry off the rubber casing with my beak and try to break into someone's conversation and yell 'nine-one-one!'"

"By then he'll have bitten my head off and snapped my bones," said the mockingbird.

"Quite possibly so," said the cat. "All this interesting conversation is making me feel a bit peckish."

"This is a tough one," said Little Red Robin

Hood. "I can't think what to do. There's too much music going on in the forest this afternoon. It's hard for a superhero to concentrate."

"What *is* that noise?" said the mockingbird. "It sounds like horns."

Suddenly Little Red Robin Hood had an idea. "It *is* horns," he said, "and that means a hunt is going on! The humans and hounds are chasing a fox! Mockingbird, make the sound of a fox, and the hounds will come!"

"I don't like hounds any more than I like cats," said the mockingbird.

"Do what I say!" called Little Red Robin Hood. "We have no time to lose!"

So the mockingbird cried out, in the voice of a vixen, "Oh la, I hope those nasty hounds don't catch up with me today! I'm hiding here under this big old oak tree, safe as a bug in a rug, I *hope*!"

"Stop that," said the cat.

"Oh, what care I for the joys of life anyway," screamed the mockingbird in a foxy voice, "it's all going to end in the jaws of some hound! Here I am, boys! Come and get me!"

"Louder!" urged Little Red Robin Hood.

"Going once, going twice," screeched the mock-ingbird as the hounds came bounding through the undergrowth. The cat gulped. Quick as twitched whiskers, the cat let go of the mockingbird and bounded up the trunk of the oak tree. The mocking-bird and Little Red Robin Hood flew to the limbs of a nearby spruce tree. The hounds looked puzzled and then ran on.

"How can I ever thank you?" asked the mockingbird.

"This is a holdup. Stick 'em up," said Little Red Robin Hood.

"No, really," said the mockingbird.

"No, really," said Little Red Robin Hood. "I rob from the rich and give to the poor. And besides, you tricked me and I'm lost. Give me all your money."

"So that's why you wear a mask," said the mocking-bird. "Well, all I have is a small stock of grubs in a nearby tree. I guess I can show you where they are. I owe it to you."

The mockingbird showed Little Red Robin Hood where the grubs were. Then the mockingbird led Little Red Robin Hood back to the telephone wires, where they found the basket of goodies on the ground. Little Red Robin Hood gave the mockingbird the wormy pound cake in exchange. "So I'm not *really* robbing you," he said. "My mama would wallop me and send me to bed without any worms if she thought I was being a *real* thief."

"I hate wormy pound cake," said the mockingbird.

"Go drop it on the head of that cat then," said Little Red Robin Hood, and he picked up his basket. It was much lighter since the cake was gone; grubs hardly weigh anything.

The sun was sinking, and Little Red Robin Hood was afraid that his grandmother would be worrying about him. He hurried along. But his grandmother wasn't worrying about *anything*. No siree. That was because the cat, in a rage at having lost the mocking-bird, had streaked ahead to the apartment house where Grandma Robin lived. The cat had found the key under the mat and let himself in. He had gobbled up Grandma Robin in one big gulp. Then he dressed himself as best he could in Grandma Robin's nightie and nightcap, climbed in her bed, and used the channel changer to click off the soaps. He preferred talk shows.

When Little Red Robin Hood got to his grandmother's retirement apartment, he was surprised that the key wasn't under the mat. But he could hear the TV blaring away, and he saw that the door was unlocked. He came in and set the basket of goodies down on the kitchen table. "Yoo-hoo, Grandma," he called. "I'm here."

"Who is that?" called the cat, who had picked up a little from the mockingbird about imitating voices. "Is that the mailman?"

"No, it's your favorite superhero," cried Little Red Robin Hood, and flew through the doorway into his grandmother's bedroom.

There he stopped. "My word, Grandma," he said, "you're really *not* feeling well, are you?"

119

"No," said the cat, "I'm quite poorly, bless my whiskers."

"I never noticed you had whiskers before," said Little Red Robin Hood.

"It's a symptom of this dreadful flu," said the cat. "Instant whiskers. Most embarrassing for a bird of downy cheek, as I have always prided myself to be."

Little Red Robin Hood came a little closer. "My, Grandma," he said, "this must be a *very* bad flu. What great big pointy ears with little tufts of fur in them you have."

"The better to hear you with, my child," said the cat. "You know, your hearing goes when you get old, so the bigger ears are a help."

"Grandma," said Little Red Robin Hood, "what great big slanted eyes you have!"

"The better to see you with, my dear," said the cat, "especially when I've misplaced my bifocals again. I think I left them on the bus last week, coming back from my senior citizens' support group meeting."

"Grandma," said Little Red Robin Hood, "what a

great big tail you have poking out from under the bedsheets!"

"Surprise," said the cat. "That's not a tail; it's a furry snake puppet, but the eyes fell off. Doesn't it move realistically?" And that cat twitched his tail in a lifelike way, which wasn't hard.

"Grandma," said Little Red Robin Hood, "would you like some grubs or some wormy cheese?"

"Bless your heart, you guessed exactly!" said the cat. "But I'm too weak to feed myself. Could you just get some and put it in my mouth?"

Little Red Robin Hood obliged. He unwrapped the wormy cheese and piled some grubs on top, and flew onto the bed. "Open your mouth and close your eyes, and you shall get a big surprise," he said.

"*Someone* will get a big surprise," muttered the cat. He opened his mouth.

"My word, Grandma, what great big teeth you have!" cried Little Red Robin Hood. "Hey, wait a minute! Birds don't have teeth! Did you get dentures? I don't *think* so! I smell a scam! Help! Police! I never saw such huge teeth!"

"The better to eat you with, my fine little feathered friend!" yowled the cat, and gulped up Little Red Robin Hood, all but the mask, which he put on himself.

Then he burped a little bit and patted himself on the back. He slinked out of Grandma's apartment, taking the TV with him.

"What a noisy little twerp!" he said as he went. "It was a pleasure to eat him!"

Just then something very solid, shaped like a brick and weighing a little more than a pound, came plummeting out of the air onto the cat's head. It was the wormy pound cake.

"Bull's-eye!" chuckled the mockingbird. "Take that, you miserable creature!"

But the mockingbird was surprised to see the cat belch like a gluttonous rhino. And even more surprised when Grandma Robin and Little Red Robin Hood popped out of the cat's mouth.

"Oh, Grandma," cried Little Red Robin Hood, "are you okay?"

"Okay? I'm awful," said Grandma. "I'm hungry, I'm confused, and I'm missing my soaps. But I'm alive again. Surprise, surprise. And I need a birdbath like nobody's business. Come on, let's go home and call your mother to tell her you arrived safely. She's apt to worry."

The mockingbird flew away and took up a career doing comic impersonations on TV. Eventually he starred in his own sitcom, but it bombed in the first season and wasn't renewed.

The cat recovered. On his way home, however, he was discovered by the hounds returning from the hunt. The hounds chased the cat so far away that he never came back.

After a little wormy treat, Grandma Robin called Mother Robin on the telephone and said, "All is well, dearie."

"I had a terrible feeling something was going wrong, old darling," said Mother Robin over the phone.

"Mothers, they always worry," said Grandma. "Dearie, you have to learn to let go. Your boy is a very brave and obedient little bird, and he will do just fine. He's going to stay overnight and keep me company."

Then Grandma and Little Red Robin Hood watched the soaps and had some wormy soup and crackers, and in the evening they rented a video. It was called *Super Robin Ninja Heroes*. Little Red Robin Hood loved it, but Grandma Robin fell asleep and snored through the best parts.

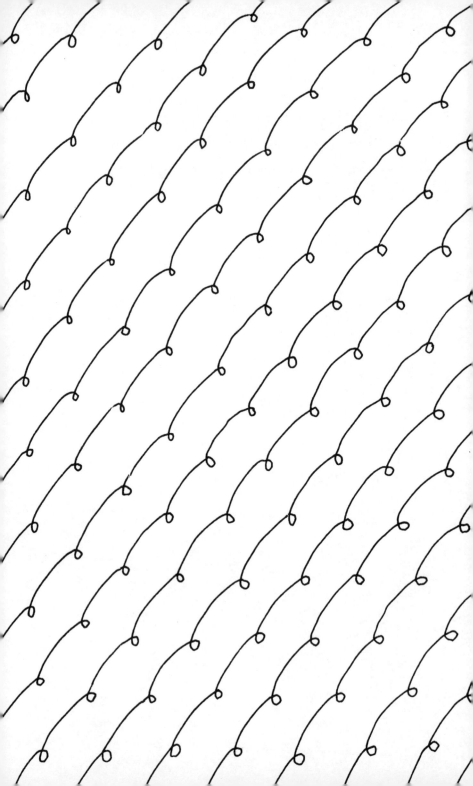

THE THREE
LITTLE PENGUINS
AND THE
BIG BAD WALRUS

Once there were three little penguins who lived in an igloo with their mother.

The oldest penguin liked to eat fish.

The middle penguin liked to eat fish.

The youngest penguin liked to get dressed up in a ballet costume and put on a show. This was not usual for penguins, and it worried old Mama Penguin a lot. But whenever her baby put on a show, she always applauded the loudest. She clapped so hard that she found herself wheezing and short of breath.

She took herself to the doctor, who was a walrus. He told Mama Penguin that her blood was sluggish. He said she should move to an island in the South Seas.

"I do feel a bit under the weather," said old Mama Penguin. "Not up to my usual strength. But what will my penguin children do without me? They haven't got a whole lot of common sense, even for penguins. They wouldn't know enough to come out of the cold unless I called them, and do you think they would floss regularly?"

"They're old enough to take care of themselves," said Doc Walrus.

"Do you really think so?" said Mama Penguin. "A mother worries."

"A mother should learn not to worry so much," said Doc Walrus firmly. "You've done a good job raising your children. It's time to let go and enjoy your happy golden sunset years. You're looking weak and frail. There's an iceberg leaving tonight. Why don't you hop aboard?"

"Perhaps," said Mama Penguin, and sighed.

She didn't intend to follow the doc's advice. But while she was away, the oldest penguin had accidentally left the oven on, and the middle penguin had accidentally left the oven door open, and the youngest penguin was skating around in baubles and bangles and beads, being Cleopatra the Queen of the Nile, not paying much attention. And while this was happening the heat from the oven had melted the igloo right down to the very tundra on which it had been built. By the time that Mama Penguin got home, there wasn't much home left to come to. So old Mama Penguin called her children to her side.

"My dears," she said, "it is time for you to go out into the world and find your own homes. As you can see, there's not much left of mine. So your dear mother is going to go on a cruise to the South Seas and try to build up her health. I'll send postcards. Meanwhile, some good advice. First, floss your teeth every day."

Then she smacked the oldest penguin on the bottom with her walking stick. "And don't leave the oven on!"

She smacked the middle penguin on the bottom, too. "Don't leave the oven door open!"

She kissed the youngest penguin and said, "Dear, a little less lipstick and it will go much better for you in life."

Then she hobbled onto a passing iceberg and soon was lost to view.

The three penguins were very sad. "What shall we do?" said the oldest penguin. "Perhaps we should build ourselves three homes. I will build my home out of straw."

"I will build my home out of twigs," said the middle penguin.

"I will make up a new dance called the Collapse of the Housing Industry," cried the youngest penguin, and began collapsing all over the place.

"Oh please," said the oldest and the middle penguins, and went to find housing materials.

Now who should come along but a seal driving a bobsled. Tied onto the back of it was a huge rick of straw.

"Straw! Straw for sale!" cried the seal.

"I'll have that straw to build myself a house," cried the oldest penguin, and bought the whole lot right there.

"I thought I was selling it for packing fine china in,

but you can do what you want with it," said the seal, pocketing the money and driving away.

The oldest penguin built a handsome house. It had a straw veranda, a straw balcony, and a straw tower perched on top. The oldest penguin was quite happy. With a new stove and a nice pot of fish to cook up on it, there was nothing more to want in life.

The middle penguin was wandering around when the seal came driving the bobsled back, this time with a load of twigs in it. "Who'll buy my twigs, fine twigs for sale!" cried the seal.

"I'll have the lot, my good seal," said the middle penguin. "Just dump them right there, if you please. This is as good a place as any to build myself a house."

"Suit yourself," said the seal. "I had thought to sell them for kindling, but you know best." The seal put the money in his wallet and drove his bobsled away.

The middle penguin built a beautiful house out of twigs. It had a twig porch, a twig staircase, and a twig

widow's walk on top. The middle penguin bought an oven just right for cooking pots of fish in, and all seemed very cozy indeed.

The youngest penguin invented a new dance called Isadora Penguin. It involved dressing in gauzy colored veils.

Along came the seal on his bobsled once again. "Coal! Lots of coal for sale!" he cried. "A very hot building material these days!"

"Who would build a house out of coal?" asked the youngest penguin. "Wouldn't it burn up?"

"I give folks what they want," said the seal. "You'd

be surprised at recent styles. You could call it a warming trend."

"Well, what I would like is a full-length mirror," said the youngest penguin. "I need to see myself dance so I can know if it's beautiful enough."

"I can't sell you a mirror, for I haven't got one," said the seal. "But I can sell you a blowtorch. You can cut a sheet of ice out of the glacier. That'll do for a mirror."

"I suppose you're right," said the youngest penguin. "Here's the money."

"Thanks," said the seal. As he handed over the blowtorch, he added, "Your eyelashes are awfully long and curly for a penguin."

"Is that a compliment?" said the youngest penguin, and practiced using the blowtorch in the seal's direction. The seal and the bobsled sped away very quickly.

Who should come along next but Doc Walrus.

The truth needs to be told. It is bitter and it is ugly, but so was the walrus.

The cunning old doctor wanted to eat all three of the penguin children. That was why he had advised poor Mama Penguin to move to the South Seas. Her blood wasn't really as sluggish as the doctor had said. It was all a fiendish plot to provide him with fresh penguin steaks.

Far away, as her iceberg began to melt in the heat of the tropical seas, old Mama Penguin was wondering if she had made the right decision. But didn't all children need to grow up and leave home sometime?

The walrus waddled up to the house built out of straw. He was exceedingly hungry. He knocked on the front door and said, "Little penguin, little penguin, let me come in."

The oldest penguin looked out the peephole. "Why are you carrying a knife and a fork and a jar of salsa?" he asked.

"I bought them at a garage sale," said the walrus. "I've come to check your pulse. Your mama told me to look in on you from time to time. I need to make sure you're flossing regularly. So let me come in."

"Not by the hair of my chinny chin chin," said the penguin.

"You haven't got any hair on your chinny chin chin," said the walrus.

"That's what I mean," said the penguin, and slammed the peephole shut.

"Then I'll huff and I'll puff and I'll blow your house in," said the walrus.

The walrus couldn't really blow the house in. He wasn't good at huffing and puffing, just bluffing. Besides, the penguin was too busy heating up a pot of fish to pay attention.

Unfortunately, the penguin left the oven on and the door open, and the house of straw went up in flames.

The penguin just barely escaped through the back door, and he ran to the house of twigs, which was nearby.

"Save me!" cried the oldest penguin.

"Oh, okay," said the middle penguin. "Would you stir these fish while I go answer the doorbell?"

It was the walrus again. "It's the good old kindly doc who makes house calls," said the walrus through the screen door. "I've come to take your temperature. And I have to check to see if you're flossing as you should. Your mama told me to keep an eye out for your health, and I intend to."

"Then what are you doing with that paring knife and the sack of onions and the sprigs of fresh coriander?" asked the middle penguin.

"I'm on my way to a cooking class over at the community college," said the walrus. "At this rate, I'm going to be late. So little penguin, little penguin, let me come in."

"Not by the hair of my chinny chin chin," said the middle penguin.

"You haven't got any hair on your chinny chin

chin," said the walrus. "Come to think of it, you haven't got much of a chinny chin chin, either."

"That about settles it, then," said the middle penguin, and slammed the door.

"Then I'll huff and I'll puff and I'll blow your house in," said the walrus.

"Enough with this huffing and puffing stuff," called the oldest penguin. But meanwhile, the middle penguin had left the oven on and the door open. The house of twigs caught fire and burned to the ground. The two penguins barely escaped with their lives.

They raced next door.

The youngest penguin had been having fun with the blowtorch. It was easy to use it to slice blocks of glacial ice into huge cubes. The youngest penguin had built a dance studio with a full wall of mirrors and a café and a lounge, complete with a jukebox all made of ice. The youngest penguin was busy perfecting an ensemble piece to go in the ballet about Cleopatra the Queen of the Nile. This number was called the Dance of the Sugarplum Pharaohs.

"Let us in!" cried the oldest penguin and the middle penguin.

"Did you come to see the show?" asked the youngest penguin. "It's not finished yet, but I can show you what I have so far."

"There's a hungry walrus outside," cried the other penguins. "Whatever you do, don't answer the door!"

Just then there was a knock. "Who is it?" called the youngest penguin, looking through the French doors.

"It's me, old Doc Walrus," said the walrus. "I've come to give you an examination."

"I'm fine," said the youngest penguin. "Go away. I'm busy flossing my teeth."

"You look as if you have a fever. Your cheeks are cherry red."

"It's a little blush. Arctic Evenings. Use a flesh-colored foundation and blend well. You should try some."

"Let me in and I will."

"But why are you carrying a meat cleaver and a hibachi?"

"I'm delivering them to my granny, who is sick in

bed. She's fading fast. Little penguin, little penguin, let me come in."

"Not by the hair of my chinny chin chin."

"You haven't got any hair on your chinny chin chin," said the walrus.

"Let me check the prop department and I'll get back to you," said the penguin. But by now the walrus had had enough. He was very hungry indeed. He found the blowtorch that the littlest penguin carelessly had left lying around outside. Then Doc Walrus aimed it at the dance studio made of carved ice.

"I'll have penguin patties before the night is out!" he cried, and turned on the blowtorch.

Meanwhile, old Mama Penguin's bad feeling about this whole business had only gotten stronger. She had turned around. She arrived at the front door of the dance studio just in time to see the walrus start to attack the building with fire.

"Oh no, you don't," she yelled, and launched herself through the air.

The walrus never knew what hit him. He was out

cold, with little *X*'s in his eyes and birdies tweeting over his head, just as in the cartoons.

"My babies!" cried old Mama Penguin, calling them to her side.

"Mama!" they said, clapping their flippers. They came sliding over the ice to her. "How did you ever knock out that old walrus?"

"My blood isn't as sluggish as all *that*," she said. "Besides, as the iceberg began to melt, I had to paddle it all the way home against the current. I built up my upper body muscles. A little exercise does wonders, my

dears. But enough about me. Tell me this, my children. Has anyone left the oven on and burned up any houses lately?"

The oldest penguin and the middle penguin hung their heads in shame. The youngest penguin said, "Look, Ma, I can do a split now," and showed her how.

"My baby," said Mama Penguin fondly. "I guess I'll have to move back in and do the cooking. Nobody touches the oven or I'll spank you on your bottoms. Understood?"

"Yes, Mama," they said.

They tied up the walrus with dental floss. When the seal with the bobsled came along, they piled the walrus on top and told the seal to take him away to the county jail. Then old Mama Penguin made some fish soup for dinner, and the oldest penguin and middle penguin told her how beautiful their houses had been.

The youngest penguin worked on a new dance, called the Ice of Spring. It was intended to be danced, daringly, in the nude, but since penguins don't usually wear clothes, nobody especially noticed the difference.

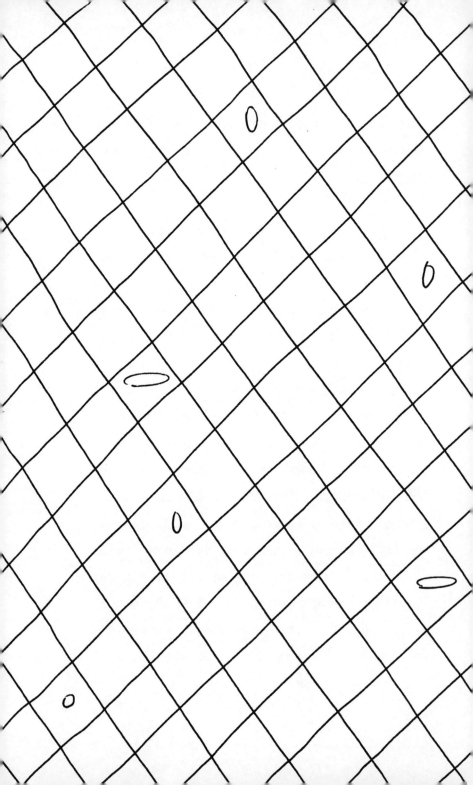

CINDER-ELEPHANT

In a far-off land there lived a king and queen whose lives seemed perfect. They had a terrific castle filled with the latest conveniences. They had a royal box at the soccer matches. They had season tickets to the symphony. But none of this could make them happy.

"If only I could have a child, my life would be fulfilled," said the queen, sighing. "What good is a castle without the sound of children laughing with joy? What good is a royal box for the soccer games without the sound of children screaming with excitement? What good is a season ticket to the symphony without the sound of children snoring with boredom? Besides, all those violins, they make me feel seasick."

"You *have* been looking pale lately," said the king. "You should see a doctor."

The queen went to the outpatient clinic. The doctor

was a kindly kangaroo. "So what seems to be the problem?" she asked.

"I want to have a child," said the queen. "And so does the king."

"You have too much stress in your life," said the kangaroo doctor. "It's not easy being a queen. Put your feet up. Get out more. Go to the symphony or something."

"I hate the symphony," said the queen, and started to weep.

"There, there," said the kangaroo doctor. "I have just the thing. A little tea brewed just for you." She bustled about her office and made a nice pot of hot tea. She served the tea in a cup shaped like an elephant head, with a handle formed out of the curving trunk.

"All will be well," said the kangaroo doctor. "You'll see. Here's my card. Call me if you've any news."

"I will," said the queen, feeling better, and she took a cab home.

In time the queen found herself growing a little stouter. At first she thought it was because she had stopped going to the symphony and the soccer games. She wasn't getting much exercise. But when the king said, "My dear, you're glowing with health," the queen finally realized the reason.

"We're going to have a baby!" she cried. So she sent the kangaroo doctor a little note of thanks, and a box of chocolates besides.

For many months the queen grew larger and larger. In fact, she grew a good deal larger than anyone expected. The kangaroo doctor had to make a house call—that is, a castle call. "Looks like you're going to have about eight or ten little babies," said the kangaroo doctor. "Either that, or one really big one."

"My goodness," said the queen.

"Well, you wanted a baby," said the kangaroo doctor.

"I shall love it—or them—*all* of them," said the queen firmly. "I have never been happier."

The king said devotedly, "You have never looked lovelier."

The kangaroo doctor said, "You have never looked *larger.*"

At last the baby was due. The queen's maids-in-waiting and the kangaroo doctor came by to assist. They were surprised when they delivered a beautiful little baby elephant. Well, little for an elephant. When the queen saw her, she wept tears of joy. "I have a child at last, and I have never been happier!" she cried. Then—in that horrible ricocheting way of stories such as these—she died.

The king went nearly blind with grief. The kangaroo doctor hopped away, too sad to speak. The maids-in-waiting called the baby Ella, put her in a cradle the size of a bathtub, and sang her to sleep.

Now, the king mourned the loss of his beloved wife for many months. He found it painful to look at Ella, for she reminded him of his dead queen. In the end he quit his job as king and took a new job as a bus driver, which was pretty hard to do because he was mostly blind. But no one liked to criticize his driving because they knew of the sadness he had been through. His regular customers on the Number 72 bus found themselves miles away from where they wanted to be. They had to get new apartments and take new jobs on a regular basis.

In time the bus driver married a new wife. She was not much to look at, but then he didn't have much to look at her *with*. She had two daughters from a previous marriage. They were spiky and disagreeable sorts, but they were human beings, not elephants. They made fun of their new stepsister. They called her Cinder-Elephant, for they made Ella sleep in the cinders of the kitchen fire and do all the household chores besides.

Cinder-Elephant was too devoted to her father to complain. Anyway, soon there was no father to complain to, because one day, by accident, her father drove his bus off an ocean cliff. His only passengers were seals, who fortunately could swim away to safety, but the Number 72 bus and her father drifted out of sight into the briny deep.

"Humph!" said Cinder-Elephant's stepmother when she heard the news. "Another husband takes the plunge. My first husband toppled into a well. Men are so clumsy. Well, Cinder-Elephant, no use weeping those huge tears; you're making a mess on the floor. What's done is done. Go downstairs to the kitchen and make some brownies, why don't you. I always feel a powerful hunger when I lose a husband."

Cinder-Elephant went to the kitchen and made some brownies. Because her ears were large, she could hear her stepmother and stepsisters chatting in the parlor overhead.

"I don't like that Cinder-Elephant," said the older stepsister, whose name was Mildew. "Those tusks give me the creeps."

"And that trunk!" shrieked the younger stepsister, whose name was Mayhem. "Talk about needing a nose job!"

"*She'll* never get a husband," agreed the stepmother. "Which is lucky for us, as it's nice to have our own private pastry chef. Now, my dears, listen to me. I know we've got to plan a memorial service for that sadly departed bus driver fellow. But first, the important things. The mail has arrived, and here is an envelope directed to 'All the Fair Maiden Occupants' at this address. It seems that the new king and queen, the ones who were hired to take over from the old ones, are having a ball. I hear through the grapevine that they have a son of marrying age. He is looking for a wife. I suggest the three of us go and present ourselves with our best foot forward."

"My feet are dainty," said Mildew. "Your feet have fallen arches."

"*My* feet are dainty," said Mayhem. "Your feet are smelly."

"Girls, don't argue about the virtue of your feet," said their mother. "In a beauty pageant my feet would stomp all over yours every time, but never mind about that. My dears, we must primp and preen. One of us must be the prince's bride. I hope it will be me, as I am newly available. But if it is either of you, I demand the best room in the castle. I demand tickets to the soccer games. But I'll skip the symphony, as I prefer yodeling to myself in the privacy of my own bathroom."

Cinder-Elephant wept bitter tears into the mixing

bowl. She missed her father, and she feared that no prince would ever select her, even if she got to *go* to the ball. Which she doubted would happen.

That evening she brought up the subject while she was clearing the table of soup bowls.

"May I go to the ball with you?" she said.

"You've been eavesdropping again, you nosy thing," snarled Mildew.

"Nosy! *I'll* say nosy!" Mayhem pointed at Cinder-Elephant. "Look at the shnozzola on you! What prince would ever want to kiss *you*?"

"These brownies are too salty," said the stepmother. "Have you been weeping into the brownie batter again?"

"I was sad today," said Cinder-Elephant, nodding her huge head. "I miss my father. And I want to go to the ball."

"The only ball you'll ever go to is the one you'll balance on when I sell you to the circus!" cried the stepmother. She threw the brownies into the fireplace. "Now get back to the kitchen and bake us each a pecan pie! Pronto! We're not leaving this table till we get some decent dessert!"

"And if you cry into the batter this time, we'll send you back until you get it right," said Mayhem.

"While we're waiting, let's plan our gowns for the ball," said Mildew.

Cinder-Elephant said, "If I make perfect pecan pies, may I go to the ball, please?"

"We'll see," said the stepmother. "I can't decide now; I'm having a sugar low."

Cinder-Elephant got out three glass pie dishes and molasses, sugar, and nuts. She slaved over the hot oven and made three pecan pies. But when she delivered them, her stepmother still refused to give an answer.

"Tomorrow you can make us some mince pies. If they're *very* good, I'll decide then," she said.

In the days that followed, the stepmother and stepsisters chose fabric for their ball gowns. They engaged a zebra seamstress to cut and sew for them. Every night Cinder-Elephant presented new pies: deep-dish cherry pie, Boston creme pie, lemon chiffon pie, key lime pie, pear and ginger pie, peach and pineapple pie, and mock apple pie, made with Ritz crackers and a little lemon juice. However good the pies were, the stepmother decided they were never good enough. "You'll never catch a man if you're no good in the kitchen, Cinder-Elephant!" she cried. "Try again! Tomorrow we want blueberry-and-currant pie!"

Once a week the zebra seamstress had to come and rip out the seams of the ball gowns. With all these pies, the stepsisters and stepmother were putting on a little weight.

Finally the evening came for the ball. The stepmother had almost run out of ideas of pies to ask for. They'd had Georgie-Porgie-pudding-'n'-pie. They'd had Jack-Horner's-thumb-in-the-Christmas-pie. They'd had four-and-twenty-blackbirds-baked-in-a-pie. "Give us three good old pumpkin pies," said the stepmother at last, waddling out of the kitchen. "If they are tasty enough, you may go to the ball. Though what you'll wear I hardly dare think! Maybe you can sew the curtains into a dress! That'll be large enough! Ha-ha-ha!"

Cinder-Elephant had an enormous pumpkin delivered under the linden tree in the kitchen yard. She was sharpening a carving knife to cut it with when Mayhem and Mildew came thudding down the steps into the kitchen. The stepsisters got stuck in the kitchen doorway and then barreled through.

"Oh la, Cinder-Elephant's cooking again!" cried Mayhem. "Don't I look elegant in my ball gown?" She spun around. Dressed in cherry-colored fabric, Mayhem looked a bit like a dancing sofa.

"I look better!" shrieked Mildew. In emerald green, she resembled a cavorting refrigerator overgrown with moss.

Mayhem picked up a jar of allspice from the table where Cinder-Elephant had put it, ready to use in her nightly baking. Mildew grabbed it from her and shook it in the air toward their stepsister. "Happy baking, you clot!" they chorused.

Then looks of horror crossed their faces as they saw

Cinder-Elephant's eyes close and her nose twitch.

"A sneeze!" cried Mayhem.

"Oh please!" cried Mildew.

"She's going to blow!" cried their mother, looking down the steps into the kitchen. "Run for your lives, girls!"

Elbowing past each other through the doorway, the stepsisters almost did each other in. Cinder-Elephant, her nose tickled by the dust of allspice, sneezed so massively that she fell against the fireplace and was knocked out cold.

When the stepmother looked down a few minutes later, she said, "No pumpkin pies, I see, and lazy Cinder-Elephant is snoozing by the fire again. She doesn't deserve to go to the ball with us. Come, daughters. Let us step lively and win ourselves a prince."

When Cinder-Elephant came to, she realized that the house was quiet and her stepfamily had deserted her. Though she didn't believe in feeling sorry for herself, it was all too much this evening. First her mother had died in childbirth, and then her almost-blind father had driven his bus off a cliff into the sea. How much worse could life get?

Still, there was work to be done. She would mind her manners until she was old enough to get her own flat in town. Maybe then she could open a bakery or something.

Trying not to cry, she decided to carve up the pumpkin and remove the seeds. But she couldn't help uttering one quiet sob. "Oh, if only someone kind could help me!"

To her immense surprise, someone appeared. At first Cinder-Elephant thought it was a beautiful spirit, but then she realized it was a kangaroo wearing a stethoscope. She had bounded through the kitchen window.

"I just happened to be wandering by," said the kangaroo doctor, for it was she. "I attended your birth, dear girl, and though you never knew it, I have always made it my business to be sure you were all right. Why are you crying?"

"I wanted to go to the ball," said Cinder-Elephant. "But I didn't make any pumpkin pies."

"So who needs pumpkin pies tonight?" said the kangaroo doctor. "They're having fresh fruit and yogurt at the ball, very healthy and low in calories. Why don't you just go?"

"I have no gown," said Cinder-Elephant.

"Well, I'm no fairy godmother," said the kangaroo doctor, "but I happen to have in my pouch a couple of hospital robes. And I've had a lot of experience stitching up wounds, so I could quickly stitch up a gown. Will that help?"

"You're so kind," said Cinder-Elephant. "But how shall I get there?"

"Look at that pumpkin," said the kangaroo doctor. "I'm no fairy godmother, but I happen to have in my pouch some spare axles and four huge wheels. I do auto repair in my spare time. It's not all that different from surgery. Could we affix the pumpkin to these wheels? Then we could hitch it to the horses tied up out front."

"I thought the horses took my stepmother and

stepsisters to the ball," said Cinder-Elephant.

"They had to walk. The horses couldn't drag all three of them," said the kangaroo doctor. "The horses would have keeled over with cardiac arrest. But they could manage pulling *you*. Though you need to exercise more, dearie. Lose a few pounds. Dance up a storm tonight."

"I have no shoes!" cried Cinder-Elephant suddenly.

"Do I have to think of everything?" said the kangaroo doctor. "I want to be helpful, but there's a limit. Do you think I carry a full line of Italian footware in my pouch? Use your noggin, my dearie. You're a bright girl."

Cinder-Elephant looked around the room. She found two of the glass pie plates she had been about to use for pumpkin pies. They were just about the same size as her feet.

"Perfect! Glass slippers!" cried the kangaroo doctor. "You'll have to dance carefully, my dear, or I'll be pulling slivers of glass out of your heel from now till dawn. Now off you go to the ball. One word of advice, though. Leave by the stroke of midnight. Nothing much will happen if you don't, except that the pumpkin carriage will start to rot after a while. You don't want the prince to see you leaving his fancy party in a coach smelling of decaying vegetable matter."

Cinder-Elephant kissed the kangaroo doctor and jumped in the pumpkin carriage. Off she rode to the ball.

By the time Cinder-Elephant arrived at the castle, the party was in full swing. There was a forty-piece band playing sambas and polkas. On the buffet tables was lots of fresh fruit, and not a pie in sight. And the prince, standing in a bored manner behind the throne picking a shred of orange from between his two front teeth, was the most handsome thing Cinder-Elephant had ever seen.

Cinder-Elephant came through the door into the ballroom. All eyes glanced up at her.

"Who's that ravishing beauty?" said the king. "What a big healthy girl!"

"Look at that exquisite nose!" said the queen. "How marvelous!"

"That vamp! Now I see that white is the best color

for a gown, not cherry or emerald!" cried Mildew.

"That hussy! Those glass slippers are to *die* for!" cried Mayhem.

"Girls, keep your voices down; you sound shrill and vain," said their mother.

Cinder-Elephant descended the main staircase slowly, elegantly, taking care not to crush the pie plates. In one bound the prince cleared the ballroom and knelt at the foot of the stairs. "May I have the honor of this dance?" he cried.

He swept her in his arms—or as much of her as he could hold. Around the dance floor they swirled.

Mildew turned green with envy, matching her gown. Mayhem blushed cherry with rage, matching her gown. Their stepmother nibbled on a slice of melon and wished the castle kitchens were serving pie.

All night long the prince danced with Cinder-Elephant. He had eyes for no other. Beyond that, he was actually an interesting guy. He had a comic book collection second to none in the kingdom, and he knew a lot about music. "Do you like soccer play-offs?"

he murmured into Cinder-Elephant's ear. "I have tickets to the royal box."

Too soon, the clock struck twelve. Cinder-Elephant, remembering the kangaroo doctor's warning, tore herself away from the prince's fond embrace and lumbered to the doorway. "Wait! Come back! I didn't get your phone number!" cried the prince. But Cinder-Elephant had already begun to ascend the stairs, and she found it hard to change direction once she had got herself going.

The kangaroo doctor's advice had been sound. The pumpkin coach was already beginning to sag on its chassis. "Hi, ho, and away!" cried Cinder-Elephant, and the carriage rumbled away, leaving a trail of pumpkin seeds behind. Cinder-Elephant was halfway home when she realized that in her haste, she had lost one of her glass pie plates.

The prince, meanwhile, had followed his beloved as quickly as he could. He saw a huge pumpkin trundling off into the distance, which was surprise enough. But when he saw the pie plate on the castle steps, he knew he had a clue to the identity of his sweetheart.

165

The next day the prince issued a proclamation. He would search the kingdom over and find the one whose foot fit into a glass pie plate.

Back at their home, Mildew and Mayhem tittered with hope. They had stuffed themselves with so much pie in the previous weeks that their feet were swollen. With a little care, one of them might yet nab that handsome prince as a hubby!

Within the hour the prince was hot on the chase. All he had to do was follow the trail of pumpkin seeds. It led straight to the house of the stepmother, stepsisters, and Cinder-Elephant.

"May I see if the feet of any females present fit into this pie plate?" asked the prince. "I know it's a rude thing to ask, but I'm looking for someone to be my bride. In between fittings, I promise to wipe the pie plate clean with this cloth."

The stepmother went first. Her foot looked a little bit like a blanched cod in the dish. Its toes flopped out over the lip of the pie plate. "No, I think not," said the prince.

Mayhem went next. Her foot spread to either side

of the pie plate, but her toe and heels were short of the rim by an inch or more. Unless she applied a strong glue, there was no way this pie plate would ever stay on her foot.

"Sorry," said the prince. "Not that you haven't got a lovely foot, in a ploppy sort of way."

Mildew went last. She had pounded her own foot with a hammer to make the arch fall and to make her foot swell with purple bruises. Her foot almost fit. Her sister and her mother held their breaths. The prince looked confused. "I don't remember your foot so purple," he said, trying to buy time to think.

"I danced with you for so long last night," said Mildew cleverly. "I have experienced a little discomfort today. Nothing serious."

"Shall I call the doctor?" said the prince. "I wouldn't want my bride-to-be to suffer."

"No need to call, here I am," said the kangaroo doctor, bounding through the open window with a single leap. "My, that's a nasty foot. I'll have to amputate." And she took out a surgical saw from her pouch.

Mildew withdrew her foot from the pie plate and she sat on her foot. "You'll do no such thing, you beast!" she cried.

Just then a smell of pumpkin pie came wafting from the kitchen. "Is there someone else in the house?" said the prince. "Someone you may have forgotten about?"

"No," said the stepmother. "Nobody."

"Some servant girl?"

"Nope. Not a soul," said Mayhem.

"Some visiting friend? Some beggar woman in the kitchen, gnawing on a bone that in your charity you've thrown her?"

"Fat chance," said Mildew. "Any bones that need gnawing on, we gnaw ourselves."

"Then whence the smell of pumpkin pie?" cried the prince.

"That's your cue, dolly, if ever I heard one!" called the kangaroo doctor.

And because Cinder-Elephant had such good ears, she had heard every word being said in the parlor above. She appeared in the doorway dressed in hospital-robe white, wearing a pie plate on one foot and carrying a pumpkin pie with her trunk. She traipsed delicately across the parlor floor and set her naked foot into the other pie plate. It fit perfectly.

"My darling!" cried the prince.

"And I can cook, too," said Cinder-Elephant.

"Let me take you away from all this!" cried the prince.

"I have a forgiving heart," said Cinder-Elephant as she turned to say good-bye to her stepsisters and stepmother. "I forgive you all. But I am an elephant. I *never forget.*"

The prince took Cinder-Elephant off to the castle, where he introduced her to his parents. They got married and opened a bakery in the basement of the castle. Once a week Cinder-Elephant and the prince went to the symphony or the soccer matches.

And that's the end of the story, except that it turned out that Cinder-Elephant's father, who had been presumed to be lost at sea when he drove his Number 72 bus off a cliff, had actually floated away to an island. When a passing tugboat agreed to tow his bus back to the mainland, he accepted the offer. After the kangaroo doctor repaired the engine, the bus driver took up his old habits again, driving his bus wherever he chose.

One day, since he was still nearly blind, he accidentally drove over the feet of his former wife and Mildew and Mayhem, who were standing with their toes too far off the curb. At last their feet really *did* fit in glass pie plates. But by then it was too late.

RUMPLESNAKESKIN

Down by the old mill stream, there stood a mill. In the mill there worked a miller. He was a sheep named Bubba.

Now Bubba had a beautiful daughter named Norma Jean. Her fleece was as yellow as a field of dandelions. Furthermore it was naturally curly. When she went for a drink in the millpond, she tossed her flaxen locks and admired herself in a mirror. "How like a movie star I am!" she said. "If only I could be discovered!"

Norma Jean never helped her father at the mill at all. She took to sipping sodas at the local five-and-dime. She wore tight little knitted sweaters from the wool of a lesser breed. It made a nice contrast. She changed her name from Norma Jean to Beauty.

One day the king of the country came by the mill. He was a noble stag, with a rack of antlers nine feet across. "Yes, sure, I'm king," he said to the miller, "but I make movies in my spare time. I'm an auteur. I'm looking for locations to shoot a new film. I think I might just use your mill, if you let me. The sun on the water of the millpond would look very nice in the opening credits."

"What's the movie called?" asked the miller.

"It's a horror movie," said the king stag. "It's called *Beauty Ate the Beast*."

Just then Beauty came gamboling into the room. When she saw the king stag, she began to amble in an attractive way. "I loved your last film!" she breathed in a deep voice, as if she had the flu. "The critics didn't know what they were talking about! It was a masterpiece of the genre!"

"You mean *Jack the Giant Killer*?" said the king stag. "Nobody understood it."

"I lived it. I loved it. It made me laugh. It made me cry," said Beauty. "It made me glad to be a sheep."

"Everybody said it was too bloody," said the king stag. "Gee, you know a lot about films."

"Also she's very photogenic," said Bubba, who was anxious to nudge his daughter's film career along. Besides, she wasn't much use around the mill. She never lifted a hoof to help.

"I'd love to ask you to star in my new movie," said the king stag, "but I'm having trouble raising enough money to make it. Everyone's jittery since *Giant Killer* was such a huge flopperoo."

"She's good at making money, too," said Bubba, who was maybe a little *too* anxious to move his daughter's career along. For next he said, "She's a winner. She can spin straw into gold."

"No!" said the king stag. "Really?"

"I prefer not to; it ruins my nails," said Beauty quickly. But before she knew it, the king stag had arranged for her to come to his movie studio and spin some gold for him.

"Good-bye, honey," said Bubba, kissing his daughter fondly. "Spin nicely for our king."

"Are you crazy, Pops?" said Beauty. "I don't know how to spin wool, much less straw into gold."

"I didn't mean it literally," said Bubba. "I meant that any piece of trash you star in will make a bundle. But don't worry. You're clever, you'll think of something. Ta ta," said Bubba. To tell the truth, Bubba had been getting a little fed up with Beauty's vanity.

The king stag chattered all the way to the studio about camera angles and foreign rights and how genius usually ends up on the cutting-room floor. "You'll be a big star one day," he said to Beauty. "You've got the looks. You've got the curves. I've got a serious case of the nerves. Spin me some gold, sweetheart. All the world will thank you for it."

And off he went, locking the door behind him.

Now Beauty threw herself down on the floor and wept. In a corner of the room was a huge pile of straw that the king stag expected her to spin into gold. The bankers were coming in the morning to count it. "What shall I do?" she asked. "I just painted my nails this morning. I can't spin this straw. It's beneath my dignity as a soon-to-be movie star."

Suddenly she heard a rustle in the straw. Using her

back hooves so as to protect her front nails, which were colored a delicious Popsicle red, she kicked the straw away. Waking from a deep sleep was a huge cobra with two impressive fangs right where you'd expect them to be.

"What're you doing here?" asked Beauty.

"I fell asleep in a meadow and look where I am," said the cobra. "Gosh, I'm starved. And you look lovely tonight, my dear." He smiled in a hungry way.

"Well, don't get any big ideas, buster," said Beauty, "because if you come one inch nearer I'll stamp your brains all over the floor. I'm not in the mood for kissing cobras. I've got to spin this straw into gold, and how the dickens do I do that?"

The cobra said, "If I tell you how, will you give me a little kiss?"

"If you do all the work and be quick about it, I'll give you one eensy-weensy kiss," said Beauty. "And I don't promise to like it."

"What I need," said the cobra, "is some of your beautiful golden fleece. I'll just take a third—say from around your middle? It'll make you look a little like a French poodle. Emphasize your delicate waistline. They'll go crazy about the new look. You'll set a trend."

"I don't know," said Beauty, but the cobra set to fleecing her. When he was done, she looked like a sheep who had had a run-in with a lawn mower. She spent the rest of the evening putting her wool into spit curls, trying to make the best of a bad business.

But the cobra was true to his word. He spun her fleece into gold and threw the straw out the window so nobody would know. Then he came forward and Beauty gave him a lip-smacking kiss on the head. "Va va va voom," he said. "I could fall for you in a big way, sweetheart."

"Get lost, you bother me, cobra," she said. "Scramola. Vamoose." So the cobra squeezed away through a mouse hole in the baseboard.

The king stag was delighted to see the gold. He sent it off with the bankers, and they agreed to finance the film. True to his word, he hired Beauty to star in it, and she was a vision of loveliness in the scene with the guillotine and the butcher knife. But before long they ran overbudget and the bankers—a squadron of squirrels— came round to ask the king stag for some more money.

The king stag put the problem to Beauty. She told him that spinning straw into gold wasn't in her contract, and if he wasn't careful she'd walk out and leave him with unusable footage. But he locked her in a room with a heap of straw, promised her a percentage of the profits, and said he'd come back in the morning.

Beauty sat down and wept again, but after a while she kicked aside the straw just in case the cobra happened to be napping there. And what do you know, he was.

"Hello, cupcake," he said, yawning. "Do you have a feeling we are meant to be together? It's in the stars."

"Cut the baloney," she said. "I need your help."

"What will you give me?" he asked. "A little hug?"

"One little hug," she said, "a little sisterly hug, that's all. And no hugging back. I don't want to be the first nine-foot-tall sheep. The world's not ready for that."

"I'm a cobra, not a boa constrictor," he said, hurt. But he gave her a once-over and said, "This time, sweetie, it's the back legs. The fleece has got to go. Trust me. You'll thank me for it."

"You were right the last time," she said. "There isn't a ewe in the kingdom who hasn't had her midriff shaved. Slaves to fashion, the lot of them. *Sheep!* And I do have particularly shapely legs, if I do say so myself. Well, all right, I suppose it can't be helped. But be gentle, please; I'm a bit ticklish."

So the cobra fleeced the sheep from her waistline to her little bobbed tail, and then he sat and spun the fleece into straw. It might have been smart of Beauty to watch and see how it was done in case this problem happened again. But she was too busy chewing the horny parts off her fetlocks in order to display a more delicate ankle.

The cobra threw the straw out the window again and departed through the mouse hole in the baseboard. When the king stag came to collect the gold, he was delighted to find Beauty looking more splendid than ever. "A hard night's work, and you look fresh as a daisy!" he said. "And your hair, you've done something to your hair. Don't tell me. Highlights?"

"I'm half naked, boss," she said.

He was scandalized. But times were changing, so he went on with the film. The advance reports on the daily rushes were ecstatic. "Cutie Beauty Almost Nudie," cried the trade journals. Beauty could hardly go out shopping without a mob forming all around her. She took to wearing dark glasses and a huge veil made out of a flowered tablecloth.

The film was almost done. A thousand theaters across the land were eager to book it. The scenes with Beauty and the chain saw were said to reach new heights of postmodern excellence. But then there was a backlash. A crowd of concerned citizens—mostly wombats—began to protest violence and nakedness in the movies. The squirrels returned and told the king stag he'd have to reshoot some key scenes and turn it into a musical with a happy ending. The king stag stomped around for a while and ran his antlers into a few trees to release a little tension. But his career was on the line. He came to Beauty.

"The very last time, I promise," he said. "We need to shoot some extra footage and I'm out of cash. Please. Please."

"Oh, don't beg, don't ever beg. If there's one thing I can't stand, it is directors who beg," said Beauty. "I could walk right out of here, you know. I've got a little mill and a loving father waiting for me. I don't need this. I don't need you."

"Actually, you do," said the king stag, "because your father has sold the mill and moved to Tahiti. I just got a postcard."

So the king stag locked Beauty in the room one more time and sent in a load of straw. This time Beauty wasted no time trampling down the straw looking for the cobra. He was not there. She was beside herself with fright and worry. "My career is going down the drain!" she cried. "I'm too young to peak this early!"

There was a rustle—not in the straw, but in the baseboard. The cobra stuck his head out of the mouse hole.

"I actually live here now," he said. "Since the harvesters keep raking me up and dragging me here anyway."

"You've got to help me!" she cried.

"Honeypot, you *need* help," said the cobra. "Have you seen those bags under your eyes? You could fit a week's shopping in them. Not a pretty sight. If I spin your last fleece into gold, what'll you give me?"

"Oh, what do you want?" she asked. "A toaster oven? A set of encyclopedias?"

"To marry you and take you away from all this."

"Get a grip. Get real. Not in your lifetime. No way."

"Well then," he said, hurt, "how about your firstborn child?"

"Oh, anything," she said. "Just get to work."

"Now, I'll have to crop you from your lovely little chin right down to your waist," he said. "That'll leave you pretty much exposed. I hope you're ready for this."

"The climate isn't right for sheep to do nude scenes," said Beauty, "but what choice do I have? I'll get a muumuu and do character parts. Just close your eyes while you work, will you? I do have a shred of modesty left."

So the cobra fleeced the sheep, keeping his eyes closed as he promised. When he was done, he sat in a corner of the room and spun the fleece into gold. Beauty sat in the other corner and made herself a coat out of straw, as she didn't want the king stag to see her entirely naked.

"So when's your firstborn child due?" said the cobra as morning broke.

"I'm not even married yet, so don't hold your breath," said Beauty. "Now go back to your mouse hole. I'm finished with you."

"I think you're finished, period," said the cobra. "If you only knew how I loved you, you'd let me take you away from all this."

"For one thing," said Beauty, "even without a coat of golden wool, I can't fit in that mouse hole. For another thing, you bug me. Beat it. *Hasta la vista.*"

The cobra left in a bad mood. He bit his tongue and almost died of his own poison.

When the king stag came, he collected the gold and blinked several times when he saw Beauty.

"You've changed," he said. "Film life doesn't agree with you. I think it's a no go, dolly. It was great fun, but it was just one of those flings. Find a job, settle down, get out of this rat race. It's killing you. You look a hundred years older. You're washed up in this town, darling. By the way, thanks for the gold."

He left and hired a new star, a blushing pig with platinum tresses.

Beauty was ashamed of herself. Now she had lost her good looks, she had lost her father, and her only friend, the cobra, had disappeared down a mouse hole. She wandered off and got a job as a supermarket cashier.

After a while Beauty met a shelf stocker and married him. He was sweet, but he was not brilliant. He was no cobra. He was rather a boar.

A year later, when Beauty had just given birth to her first child, the king stag showed up in her supermarket.

"Cuddles!" he said. "Angel! The time is right for a comeback! I've got the financing, I've got a script. It's called *The Ugly Duckling's Revenge*. A high-concept film. Sweetheart, it's you. You've got to do it. The world needs this movie. Your public needs you. I need you."

"You're holding up the line," she said. "This is ten items only, and I think you've just handed me a dozen slices of phoney baloney. Push off before I call the manager."

But in a year her fleece had grown back in, and she was now highlighting it with silvery streaks. She had a mature look, and a little of her old vanity came back.

"Hubby, I'm off to have a career," she called to the boar, who was piling cans of tuna fish in the back of the store. "Mind the baby for me till I get back! Love you lots!" Off she gamboled.

She spent a day or two learning her lines, and an hour in front of the cameras. The king stag gushed and gushed. Then he pushed her in a room with some straw. "Do what you do best," he said, and locked the door.

But the mouse hole was boarded up, and the straw was empty of cobras, and her dull old boar was too far away. "In Hollywood," Beauty said to herself, "no one can hear you scream. What a life I lead. Maybe I can just learn to spin my own fleece into gold. How hard can it be? That stupid cobra could do it."

Just then she heard a scrabbling sound at the boarded-up mouse hole. She bit the wood away and saw the head of the cobra poke through. "We meet again," he said.

"Yes," she said, "and I was a beast last time. Sorry about that. There's this pile of straw; would you mind—?"

"For one thing, your fleece is no longer golden; it's more silvery," he said. "A kind of devaluing of the currency. But anyway, I haven't come to work," he continued coldly. "I came to collect on my debt."

"Which was . . . ?" she said. "You'll have to remind me. I'm not good with details."

"Your firstborn child," he said.

"Not Boar Junior!" she gasped.

"The same," he said.

"Over my dead body," she snapped.

"That can be arranged," said the cobra, and he opened his mouth and showed his glistening fangs.

"Oh no, I'm starring in my own private horror movie based on my own life," said Beauty. "Look, Cobra, I was young and silly last year. My head was all turned around by the attention. The lights, the glamour, the champagne, the works. You can't hold a young sheep to a foolish promise. I didn't know any better."

"A promise is a promise," he said. "I helped you; now you pay me back."

"Let's make a deal," she said. "If I can guess your name, will you let me keep my baby?"

"How could you know my name?" The cobra laughed. "You never paid attention to anyone but yourself. Sure, it'll make me laugh to see you try. I'll give you three tries. Come back tomorrow at this time. Tell me my name, and I'll let you keep your baby."

The cobra disappeared with a little wag of his tail. When the king stag came in the morning, he saw the pile of straw and no pile of gold. He said to Beauty, "Gorgeous, you're letting me down. It's not nice to let me down. I can make things very unpleasant for you in this town."

"Stow it, Rake-head," said Beauty. "I need your help. If I don't find the name of this cobra fellow, it's curtains for all of us, you hear? Curtains!" And she told the king stag the predicament she was in.

The king stag sent his minions all over the land, asking up and down and side to side the name of every cobra they could find. But most cobras tend to keep to themselves. They slither away whenever anyone comes chasing at them with a pitchfork to ask them their names. At the end of the day, the king stag had nothing to report.

Beauty waited. When the cobra came back, she said, "Is your name Rambo? Is it Dumbo? Is it Bambi? Is it Simba? Is it Zorro? Is it Fred Flintstone, for goodness' sakes?"

But none of those were the right names. The cobra said, "Tomorrow night's your second chance. Better luck then," and he slid away.

The king stag wasn't happy with how things were going. His helpers interviewed everyone who had ever even seen a cobra and got their ideas. He delivered a long list to Beauty. She looked it over and made notes. When the cobra came back the next evening, she tried again.

"Is it Poison Pete? Is it Farley Fangmeister? Is it

Diamond-Back Davey? Is it Rattlin' Joe? Is it Old Snake Eyes Himself?"

"Pitiful," said the cobra when she had exhausted all her ideas. "You're running on empty, baby." He chuckled as he wriggled away. He was beginning to enjoy this.

"We're in deep do-do," said Beauty the next day. The king stag panicked. He sent out the squirrels, the wombats, the platinum-headed pig, and all the extras he could get from central casting. Everyone ran bleeting and mooing and honking and oinking in every direction.

It was the pig who saw something interesting. Poking around in the garbage Dumpster behind the supermarket, she spied a cobra on the loading dock. He was doing a little dance in the dusk. He sang a song as he danced.

> *"Everything seems very clear,*
> *But things are not as they appear.*
> *Beneath my skin I'm not the same,*
> *And Rumplesnakeskin is my name."*

The pig thought she had never seen a dancing cobra. Still, she hurried back to the king stag and told him what she had heard.

"It's a very odd name," said the king stag. "But there's nothing left to lose at this point."

That night the cobra appeared, carrying a little baby rattle between his fangs. Beauty said, "I thought you might be a rattlesnake, making that silly noise."

"Just setting up the nursery. Need to keep Boar Junior amused," said the cobra. "You know, my dear, if you had only loved me as I loved you, we might have had a beautiful life together."

"Don't torture me," said Beauty. "This isn't one of your soppy screenplays. Besides, I love my husband the boar now. He's not a mover and shaker, but he's solid. So let's get this over with. Is your name Moe?"

"No," said the cobra.

"Is it Larry?"

"No," said the cobra.

"Is it Curly?"

"No," said the cobra.

"Is it—*Rumplesnakeskin?*"

At this the cobra reared up on the tip of its tail until it stood six feet tall, and it swelled like an inflating balloon. Beauty screamed. The king stag burst through the door carrying a sledgehammer and a poison dart gun.

But there was no need to use them. The cobra spun around like a tornado, drilling the tip of his tail into the floorboards, and suddenly his skin began to split. Just like the peel of a banana falling away, the snakeskin shimmied of its own accord to the floor. It looked like

an inner tube from an old bicycle tire. An old, rumpled snakeskin.

And emerging from the center of it, blushing with embarrassment, was her husband the boar.

"My husband the boar!" cried Beauty, and she fell on him with kisses and hugs and warm tears. "Whatever were you doing in that old rumpled snakeskin?"

"I was bewitched there," he said. "Long ago I wanted to be an actor myself, but I knew there aren't many good parts written for boars. I went to a career consultant, an old witch coyote. She turned me into a cobra but neglected to tell me that there aren't many parts for cobras, either. I couldn't change back until someone fell in love with me. But you never did."

"But when I met you, you were a boar in a supermarket!" said Beauty.

"I was just playing a part," said the boar. "I borrowed a boar costume from the wardrobe department. Beneath that hairy boar skin that you married was a silvery-diamonded cobra skin, and beneath *that* was this hairy boar skin I'm in now. Only this one is the real one. Now I'm down to my own skin at last."

"Acting," said Beauty reverently. "Don't you just love it. Now listen: why did you make me guess your name?"

"That was how the spell could be broken," said the boar shyly. "But you know, you just admitted you loved me best of all. So I think that's how the spell was *really* broken. We don't need to be movie stars to be loved. We just need to be ourselves."

"It is you I love!" cried Beauty.

"And I love you," said the boar back.

"This is so beautiful," said the king stag, sniffling. "Really. Two lovebirds reunited. I love you guys. It's just like the movies. What could be better? It's a happily ever after!"